PLAYING GUY

Playing Guy

A NOVEL BY

DEENA BOUKNIGHT

PLAYING GUY
ISBN 978-1533124340

Cover Photography: Madeline R. Knight © 2016
Cover Design, Book Design: William Baker © 2016

Light Path Publishing
4903 Westfield Road
Columbia, SC 29206

"God blessed the broken road ..."
Sela

Dedicated to my father.

ONE

"Is this Guy Jamison?" asked Dr. Steward Ledger, as nurses used surgical gauze to mop up thickening blood around the eyes, mouth, and nose of the trauma patient.

"It was," offered an EMT sarcastically. His thick tree-trunk form, reeking of smoke and cheap perfume, occupied the corner of the trauma bay at Wynee General Hospital. Perspiration beaded on his disproportionately large bald head. "That pretty boy face of his is pretty much gone. Ribs are a mess. Leg was crushed. Chest is nothin' but lacerations. Don't expect he'll be wantin' to take off his shirt anytime soon to show his packs to the ladies ... that is, if he makes it."

Dr. Ledger, concentrating on his patient, ignored the EMT's hardened comments.

Minutes before, the room was placid, reposed. Briny marsh smells wafted in on the balmy night air and settled themselves in the sterile room. The nurses, Dr. Ledger, interns, and technicians yawned and quietly complained about the late hour. Francis, Wynee's orthopedic technician for the last 20-plus years, was giving a young, eager nurse an expressive summary of his latest RV road trip adventures with his wife. She smiled, but kept one eye on the double swinging doors. The group bantered back and forth about what was coming in. All they knew was that it was an automobile accident – a 911 call, versus a less life-threatening 811. Tension mounted as siren sounds neared. As soon as the double doors flung open and the patient was wheeled in, polite conversations between colleagues suddenly turned into frenzied demands. Controlled chaos ensued.

"It was an auto ax, right?" Dr. Ledger confirmed.

"Sure was," answered the EMT. "Tried to use a tree to stop his truck. Killed his parents in the process."

"That's enough from you!" bellowed Dr. Ledger at the EMT. "What the hell's your problem? Who are you anyway? Who is this guy?" he asked a nurse.

"New," she answered, expressionless.

An intern unlatched the wide red straps that held the patient to the emergency stretcher and threw them to the ground. In two swift motions, a nurse with a bulky pair of gleaming shears expertly stripped Guy of his soiled t-shirt, boxers, and jeans. Coins and bills scattered on the floor mixing thoughtlessly with splotches of blood and the discarded packaging that seconds earlier kept sterilized the gauze and needles. The smell of motor oil, vomit, sweat, and blood filled the room.

With the clothes removed, Dr. Ledger and his staff attempted to evaluate the extent of Guy's injuries. They cleared his spine with the on-site CT.

"Let's move him off the board. Ready 1-2-3."

"Bilateral dp pulse is weak"

"Blood pressure is 88 over 58"

"Normal sensations."

"Positive LOC at the site," offered a stocky blond female paramedic. "Then he gained consciousness for a few moments and was out again. We had a time prying him from the truck."

"Can you open your eyes, Mr. Jamison?" yelled Dr. Ledger.

No verbal response.

"Can you hear me, Mr. Jamison?"

Guy moaned loudly, gurgling from the blood in his throat.

"Suction him now!"

A few moments later, an intern stuck a needle in Guy's radial artery to measure his blood gases. The pain from the pressure elicited another moan.

"Do you know where you are Mr. Jamison?" demanded Dr. Ledger.

Again, no verbal response.

"Blood in both nares."

"Nose is broken. Left femur grossly unstable. Francis!"

"Already on it," said a tall, graying black man. He brought out a metal brace to secure the underside of Guy's leg; he carefully wrapped wide nylon straps around the mangled flesh.

"Breath sounds diminished on left side."

"Oxygen saturation below 82 percent!" shouted the intern measuring blood gases.

"Hemothorax!" yelled Dr. Ledger. "Hook up that chest tube and suction him. We need to find out where that blood's coming from. Did someone call Dr. Vorgate? Call and wake him. We'll need him for this leg. And call Dr. Ross just in case. Let's get a CT on him first. Could have a subdural."

Abruptly, Guy opened widely his eyes and stared at the room full of medical experts. *I don't remember this script.* His eyes latched, transfixed, on the consuming brightness of overhead lighting as his brain searched for an answer as to why he could possibly be lying on a gurney in a hospital. The nerve endings connected sharply with his brain and his face contorted with pain. He struggled to draw breath from the weight of it.

"Mr. Jamison ..." said Dr. Ledger. "Mr. Jamison, can you hear me?"

Guy winced and closed his eyes again. His breath sucked into his gut and lingered there. What he saw in his mind's eye was a foggy movie-trailer-like version of recent events: a blonde with red lipstick ... black leather sofa ... parents in the car ... *a wolf.*

"My parents," he scarcely whispered. It felt as if something thick inside his throat prevented him from speaking. He wheezed and gasped for breath. His lids opened and his eyes rolled back slightly, lashes fluttering, before he succumbed to darkness again.

"We're going to need to clear his airways!" said Dr. Ledger to his staff. "Don't try to talk anymore," he directed to Guy, who again forced open his lids. "You've sustained major injuries and we're assessing the damage."

"They're dead," said the EMT, coldly, staring straight into Guy's pleading eyes. A fleeting grin and then: "There's nothin' left of your parents now, Mr. Bad Boy Jamison!"

"Out! Right now! I want you out!" roared Dr. Ledger. "No, stop! What is your name?"

The EMT shrugged, smirked behind a wide, unkempt mustache, and sauntered out of the double doors, leaving them swinging on creaky hinges as Dr. Ledger called after him, "I will be speaking to your supervisor!"

"Unbelievable!" he mumbled loudly to no one. "He's done here! That was the last time he'll ever be allowed back into this hospital!"

Dr. Madeline Walker entered frantically through the stern metal doors; hinges screeched like faulty car brakes. She marched toward a plump nurse, holding out both her hands for sterile gloves. The nurse looked at Dr. Walker disapprovingly and then wide-eyed at Dr. Ledger. Dr. Ledger shook his head.

Maddie ... I mean, Dr. Walker, you *do not* need to be in here! I want you out! We've got it under control!"

She ignored Dr. Ledger's command. Maddie stepped toward Guy and leaned over his swollen and lacerated face. "LOC?"

"He's in and out," said a nurse.

"Guy?" Maddie whispered in his ear.

"We're going to have to intubate him," said Dr. Ledger. To the nurse he directed: "Give him 100 mgs of Propofol."

At that moment, Guy's eyes yearned to open. He knew the voice. He gurgled, struggling for breath.

"He was conscious a moment ago and that buffoon of an EMT told him his parents were killed," asserted Dr. Ledger, adding, "He's in bad shape, Maddie. There's no time right now!"

Ignoring the directive, Maddie leaned closer toward Guy. She wanted to touch his face, his hand, his arm, to give him some assurance that she was there – *really there* with him. But every fragment of him seemed saturated in a mixture of blood and dirt. Her eyes, welling with tears, connected with his glazed, bewildered expression. She moved her mouth near his ear: "They're gone, Moses. They're gone. I'm so sorry."

Maddie righted herself. She stepped aside to allow Dr. Ledger to proceed.

Guy found himself looking at what seemed to be the back of thick black velvet curtains. A memory of his first school play, his parents in the audience, crept inside and lingered for a slight moment. He remembered never wanting the curtain to close ... to see his parents' proud faces, and the admiring expressions of all the others in the audience. But this curtain closed down coffin-like, heavy, and suffocating. There was nothing. Only darkness.

TWO

GUY OLIVIER RHETT BUTTS's parents named him to be a movie star. Simple as that. They could not do anything about the last name. Some ancient Brit in the first century used the word to describe a thickset person and it stuck around for 19 more centuries. But his parents bestowed on him a first and a few middles to choose from so that when he did get to Hollywood – and they had no doubt he would end up there – he would not have to fish around for some obscure name that did not mean anything to anyone. They assumed that when he did become a movie star, the last name would be the first to go. Just plan ahead is what they figured they'd do. Rhett came from their mutually favorite character in their beloved movie, *Gone With the Wind*. They chose Olivier because they adored the actor Lawrence Olivier, especially in that film about the Sahara Desert. And the name Guy, just because.

Guy's parents, Charlene and Lawrence, loved movies – a little *too* much some residents of the town of Wynee (pronounced y-knee), South Carolina were known to have said. They met when he was 18 and she was 17 and the movie *Casablanca* had just been re-released. They stumbled into love with one another late one spring evening in Morristown, N.J. Charlene was at the movie theater with two girlfriends; Lawrence's parents were drinking again, so he had grabbed his kid brother, Mike, and dragged him to the "sissy" movie, even though he vehemently complained on the way there – and continued his lament in audible whispers during the entire movie. Leaving the theater, Mike tripped and spilled his remaining Coke Cola on Charlene's loafers. Seizing the opportunity to flirt with a girl, Lawrence pulled paper towels out of the men's restroom and carefully mopped up the spilled soda, making sure he dabbed the wetness from her exposed calves as well. Charlene smiled awkwardly, straining to suppress a nervous giggle. Groping for a snatch of a real conversation, Lawrence told Charlene that she had Katharine Hepburn qualities; she laughed loudly and shared that he had Humphrey Bogart's eyes. He asked if he could take her home. With a playful glance, she dismissed her friends. He hurried his brother home. Beginning that night, Lawrence and Charlene's relationship was sealed in the abstract. Their shared affinity for older movies, especially, became the framework for their relationship and their lives.

Charlene's exuberance excited him. To him, she had a Doris Day personality and Natalie Wood good looks. She decided he was her Jimmy Stewart: passionate in spirit, but practical and humble. She imagined him as someone with whom an interesting, but faithful and predictable relationship could be assembled.

When they celebrated, it was with dinner and a movie. When they quarreled, they compared their circumstances to those of leading characters in movies. And when they romanced one another, it was always with a quote or an allusion from a favorite film.

Even when Lawrence proposed, it was with lines from *Singin' in the Rain* because he also likened Charlene to having a Debbie Reynolds' nature – "spunky and flirty" he would tell her. He pretended to sing, dancing around her like Gene Kelly. "You were meant for me, and I was meant for you." Without hesitation, Charlene dramatically wilted in his embrace, fluttered her lashes, and responded, "I'm lucky in your arms!"

At their wedding, Charlene put her hair up in an Audrey Hepburn *Breakfast at Tiffany's* do and decided it was her one day to play the ultimate role. For their evening wedding, she dressed glamorously in white satin with delicate beading and borrowed her grandmother's white fox collared wrap for later. When they arrived at the reception, Lawrence smiled at her, took her arm, and whispered, "Let's walk down the lane with a happy refrain!"

Their lives began cheerfully and blissfully in Technicolor, but over time digressed into the somber black, white, and grays of moody Hitchcock films. Marriages do that sometimes, in film and in real life, when one spouse or both become disillusioned, bored, covetous, or gallant. The Butts's marriage suffered eventually from the latter.

But before all that, when bliss still bonded them, they moved to Wynee on a whim after Lawrence was offered a job teaching history and political science at a small, but elite boarding school – Riley Hall – catering to children from wealthy Southern families disenchanted with educational opportunities in their limited communities. They desired an adventure outside their staid New Jersey. Still relatively new as an educator, Lawrence embarked, romantically, on a mission to instill confidence and knowledge in the offspring of bankers, store owners, lawyers, and doctors. The South's youth, especially, needed educating. He planned to do his best. Charlene defined her charge as thus: the utilization of skills as a baker's daughter to bring unrecognizable Northern delights to the cloistered South. Certainly Southerners had their divinity and banana pudding; she would give them cheesecakes and tiramisu.

They settled in as foreigners in a strange land – accepted and cared for, but never quite tranquil in their aberrant hamlet.

By the time Guy was conceived only five years after their installation in Wynee, he was to the Buttses a genuine joy in the midst of their surreal, movie-epic life. If not laundered and pressed, romance wears thin. Lawrence's academic lifestyle consumed; puffed he became with compliments from parents and students. Absorbed, he withdrew from his bride with excuses of lesson plans, research, meetings, and advising. Deteriorating attention from her husband kept Charlene elbow-deep in powdered sugar, cream cheese, and mascarpone. Instead of a Rodgers and Hammerstein *Sound of Music*-like production, their lives inadvertently strayed onto a path akin to a darker John Huston flick. They painted themselves onto Wynee's canvas, but smudged one another in the process.

Their cultural shift south also caused Charlene to sweat out much of her worldly consternation toward anything spiritual and she had, although a little reluctantly, absorbed the essence of biblical teaching. Instead of a taboo or only-on-Sundays topic, which she was used to in her native northern land, the Gospel was infused into daily Southern conversations: in the lawyer's office, with the dental hygienist, in the Piggly Wiggly checkout line, over chicken salad and sweet tea at lunch. So, naturally, her film-flickering intellect led her to surmise that Guy could be their Charlton Heston "Moses" sent to deliver a slipping marriage out of an oppressive Egypt. Miraculously, over time, Guy had just that effect on his parents' depleted relationship. Charlene witnessed her husband's countenance transformed the instant the nurse placed Guy into Lawrence's arms. The creation of Guy was a healing balm to them individually – and to their union – at a time when all seemed to be lost.

A son to raise can result in a divine awakening. Out rushed the narcissistic demeanor that had encapsulated Lawrence as a popular teacher among the prep school's youth – and some faculty. Guy was medicinal life that sent his father's intellect yearning for greater knowledge and understanding in the scriptures. Charlene was drawn by drops. Each time she witnessed her husband coddling their son, she excavated a little more condemnation from her heart and flowed into that emotional chamber some supernatural grace and mercy.

They were baptized, not with the sprinkling waters of the Catholic church in which they were both raised, but with complete Baptist-style submersion in the tepid liquid of freshwater Conversion Creek – so named for all the baptisms that took place there over the years and all the sins that were absorbed into the pluff mud of the nearby marshes. The congregation of the First Baptist Church of Wynee was in attendance along the shores. It was a baptism that certainly made both John and Jesus proud, the Buttses concurred.

Lawrence and Charlene stayed on in Wynee and raised their son in the church and showed the good people of Wynee they could be forgiven, excepted. Their born-again status, however, did little to curtail their movie-obsessed ways. Extra money earned was spent inside the Town Theater, an Art Deco-era structure with 100 seats and heavy blood-red velvet curtains that opened dramatically as if the movie airing was a life or death event. Since their conversion though, Lawrence and Charlene were careful to choose more family-friendly movies. And even though *Gone with the Wind* remained their agreed-upon favorite, they prudently explained to their Christian friends that they certainly *covered their ears* when the "d-word" exited from Rhett's mouth at the movie's iconic end.

Yet, their movie-quirkiness was not all that made assimilating difficult for the Buttses in the hospitable, pineapple-motif south. Their mildly emerging eccentricities were discussed at the barber shop or when men sat on the edge of a pier fishing while their wives knitted in lawn chairs by their sides, or at Lillie's Little Store where a sign on the roof read: "Come in. We're friendly."

As Southerners, the locals reasoned that they were used to the hardships of life drawing out the "interesting" aspects of their characters. Many ascertained that since the Buttses were Yankees, they might somehow be immune to this phenomenon. Yet, the Buttses unwittingly enlightened them to this fact: It is not the place from whence you came; it's where you end up. Their adopted Southern milieu seemed to allow for the oozing out of their peculiarities. Even though fellow Southerners might not bat an eye at one of their own displaying various idiosyncrasies, the Wyneeans honed in on the Butts's glaring curiosities simply because of their outside Northern origins.

Right off the bat, people talked about how only a couple from New Jersey could find quaintness in an old antebellum dwelling that was once converted into a full-fledged funeral home. Although in disrepair, the Buttses were drawn to their home because it was a steal as a foreclosure, but also because they thought the place exquisitely charming with its aged fossilized stone columns in the entryway and the cracked black and white marble floors. The couple had visions of a reinstated grandeur for the old home, although "grand" is not how the Wynee people would describe it now. *Unique*, maybe. Still hopeful and in love when the purchase was made, the couple had every intention of eliminating the morbid funeral home ambiance and bringing it back to a resemblance of its original state – with newness sprinkled here and there.

However, the dregs of life intervened in the form of indiscretions. Charlene was pregnant with Guy at the time her eyes were opened. Restoring the home became less of a priority. Just living, grasping, and sustaining sanity was first and foremost.

But the Buttses lucidity was frequently, albeit quietly, questioned as the townspeople watched the pair load every reachable branch on every hardwood tree in their yard with colorful bottles. Eccentricity most often fell to Charlene, but Lawrence was guilty by association. He never wanted to upset her after what he did; that, in fact, would become the pattern of their lives. Instead of a traditional, manicured lawn to reflect their Georgian-style home with four massive Corinthian columns, the grounds on sunny days were a chintzy glow of light reflecting on clear, green, and blue bottles. Charlene took to scouring yard sales and flea markets for new additions to her bottle trees. Deep cobalt blue Milk of Magnesia bottles dominated.

On the less sizeable limbs that would not sustain a glass bottle, Charlene hooked or tied some version of a wind chime – most often homemade instruments constructed with odds and ends pieces of silverware that she discovered during early Saturday morning trash-treasure hunts. She tied the handle ends of the intricate, tarnished eating accoutrements with a durable fishing line, fashioned the lines to a small block of wood, and then hung the piece on an empty tree branch. At night, when the wind blew and the moon was full, the eeriness of the yard was fodder for modern Wynee ghost tales. The fact that the Butts's home was once a funeral parlor made the telling of them that much more authentic.

After Guy left home and his parents rarely heard from him, except when a new movie he was starring in was released and he called to make certain they saw it, Charlene also took to rescuing worn-out chairs discarded to the side of the road on trash day. She faithfully set her alarm every Friday to 4:30 a.m. in order to beat out any potential competition for the roadside pickings. Squash Sumney was her most ardent rival during these weekly affairs. All the way back into slavery, Squash's family looked habitually to vegetables, fruit, and other things of nature as a picking ground for solid names. Sticking names. Names that did not get flicked off like so many specks of white lint on a black coat. Her family simply would not tolerate a Robert, Jonathan, or Caroline in the family. Those were white names. Naming meant something like picking rainbow sherbet at the ice cream parlor instead of vanilla. Her mother was named Beany, her son Mater, and so on. The only break from food or nature-related names was bestowed on Squash's daughter, Patience. Squash lacked patience waiting for the child's birth as her term extended into the forty-second week. Naming her Patience, when she finally did reveal her full head of dark, tight curls, was Squash's attempt at instilling some of that character trait, which she felt she did not possess, into her offspring.

Charlene typically rose and ventured forth a little before Squash yawned her way into the thinning darkness; Squash was not a true morning person. Squash awakened early out of necessity; work and an income beckoned, but she preferred to sleep. It was a rare Friday that Squash, forcing herself awake a little earlier than work required, felt particularly perky and competitive. One such Friday, Charlene vehemently battled her regarding an antique chair – American Chippendale style – with ball and claw feet and hand-carved scroll work. They both happened upon it at the same time, blinding one another with their headlights. Someone coming upon the scene of two vehicles almost colliding and two women – one white and one black – launching out to exclaim "Firsties!" at the same time might have anticipated an all-out skirmish.

"What you mean sayin' 'firsties'? You no more got your white-ass paw print on this here chair first than the sheriff asleep in his bed. This chair mine, lady!"

"Squash, now there is no need to use foul language. This is just a chair."

With a wide smile that indicated a few missing teeth, Squash gave in. "It's too busted up anyhows. It'll never amount to anything," she argued. "Girl, you a crazy white woman anyway." She slapped Charlene gently on the shoulder. "You ain't gettin' the next one!" She hurried into her car and screeched away into a morning mist, leaving Charlene to load the chair on her own.

Alertness in early morning darkness required Charlene to drink coal black coffee and then jump into Lawrence's green Chevrolet truck that he afforded himself when they became Southerners. Lawrence, still tucked under their down-blend comforter, would sigh. *Must be Friday.* Charlene drove slowly through all the better neighborhoods of Wynee until she spotted any type of wooden chair. It had to be made of wood. No need fooling with the plastic or fake brass ones. And once upholstery gets damp, forget it. With headlights glaring on the discarded item, Charlene would scurry out of the truck and inspect it carefully. She had a knack, she revealed to those who listened, for determining immediately whether or not it qualified for chair heaven or chair hell. Chairs granted chair heaven status were in decent shape – at least functional. Perhaps they just needed a new paint job, distressing, or sanding and refinishing to resurrect them. Charlene's chair heaven was her own personal sitting room on the first floor of the home;

the formal parlor where clients once discussed the burial arrangements of their loved ones, but where Charlene met catering clients or hosted Bible studies. The room consisted of a hodgepodge of chair styles, from Boston rockers to Captain's to Fiddlebacks and all types of Windsors. Some were delicate wisps of chairs, while others were substantial, hearty designs. It was a museum of sorts for wayward chairs. *One person's trash is another person's treasure,* Charlene expressed to the inquisitive.

Chair hell was the basement. The dank space had become a graveyard littered with the remnants of chairs that Charlene could not bear to leave in a heap with the "regular" garbage by the roadside. These chairs had seen better days. Yet, some of the chairs in chair hell did not always stay there. Occasionally, Charlene would put Lawrence on the task of "saving" a few. Like a mechanic in a junkyard, he borrowed legs and seats and spindles strewn here and there to give a no-hope chair new life. Once finished, Charlene triumphantly carried the chair upstairs into the parlor and acquainted it with the others.

"I just can't believe anyone would throw away this chair," said Charlene, each time a chair received chair-heaven glory.

"I can't believe it either, sweetheart," responded Lawrence, a little condescendingly. It was always his response. She did not seem to notice.

People said that the longer Guy stayed away, the more chairs and bottles Charlene collected.

Charlene's grace, which cancelled some of her oddities, was her ability to cook the most delectable treats and present them in such frilly ambience that no Wynee bride even considered asking anyone else to cater her affair. Charlene's cakes and petit fours were like nothing Wynee had ever experienced. Sought after was her frosting, with a touch of spice that she had not revealed to a single Wyneean, not even to the editor of the weekly newspaper who begged for the recipe to accompany an article that highlighted Charlene's abilities. And her Madeleines melted in the mouths of those fortunate enough to taste them. The fact that these dainties came out of the kitchen of a former funeral home and were made by a woman who was movie and bottle and chair-obsessed, was overlooked. Charlene's culinary talents kept her booked for months.

For a time, Lawrence's persona in Wynee was a blunt contrast to his wife's. After resigning from his teaching job at the boarding school, he foundered. Instead of personable, he was angry and misplaced. He spoke to her about returning to New Jersey. She emphatically refused. He contemplated leaving. Start somewhere new, where no one knew. Guilt would not allow it. *She was pregnant, for heaven's sake.* Lawrence writhed with ignominy. Instead of seeking forgiveness, he sunk into the deep recesses of a worn leather chair. He watched old horror movies, and sci-fi flicks – dark films. Ones he knew Charlene hated. He shut himself up in their library with a small black and white television and hid from the judgment of Wynee. He viewed his betrayal as villain-like. He was the Jack Palance character who had so harshly destroyed the trust and admiration of Joan Crawford in *Sudden Fear*. He was John Proctor in the bleak, black and white French version of Arthur Miller's *The Crucible*. At times he desired the Puritan character's salvation: blindfolded on the hanging platform.

Delivering him from the precipice was Guy's birth. It was upon seeing the child's wet head and fragile expression that he experienced God, who offered saving grace. His son illuminated his nebulous existence. Infused with hope, he abandoned thoughts of leaving. His fear of Wynee's condemnation gradually dissipated. He picked up the Bible for the first time, concentrating on passages from Genesis to Revelation. His voluminous errors were written clearly on the transparent pages. He prayed for God to show him the way. God did.

After a year of no employment, Lawrence learned that the town's magistrate, Orville Holt, who had taken care of Wynee's misguided for 15 years, died suddenly. The town needed a new magistrate. Lawrence believed himself the perfect candidate: a degree in political science and a minor in criminal justice. The selling point: a foreigner in the Southern land able to apply laws and judgments without age-old family biases. Instead of shrinking from the local society, he determined to become its pillar.

Lawrence embarked on a full-out campaign to convince the esteemed leaders of Wynee that he was the man for the job. Had not Rhett Butler convinced Atlanta that he should be welcomed into high society? Certainly his own fortitude could outweigh that of a fictional character.

Lawrence did get the job. He was appointed by the governor of South Carolina, after traveling to Columbia with a few Wyneeans to appeal to the Senate. After some training, he set about adjudicating the civil cases as well as conducting all kinds of preliminary hearings. A busy day for Wynee involved issuing search or arrest warrants. Thrilling was that rare occasion when his authority was required in a criminal case. Yet, the average conflicts consisted of issuing restraining orders in those all-too-common cases where marital bliss was lacking or non-existent.

To the degenerates who roused him in those early morning hours when nothing good, except sleep, occurs, he quoted scripture in one breath and movie lines in another. Occasionally, he was asked to preside over a former minor criminal's wedding; he shared high points of the Gospel message and snippets of his humble testimony. Often, tears were shed, and more than a few times Lawrence learned that his elocution resulted in a spiritual turning point for one soul or many present at the blessed event. Upon hearing such news, Lawrence's chest capacity expanded; his stature straightened. He looked heavenward and acknowledged God's redemption for just such occasions.

Life proceeded for Lawrence. He indulged his wife her foibles, which he understood and could not blame her for, and he loved his son unconditionally. He reflected inwardly on self-forgiveness. The town, and most importantly, his wife, seemed to have forgiven him too, although nothing is really ever forgotten altogether.

Most Wyneeans acknowledged that the Buttses added their equitable share to the town's "flavor," to put it politely. Eccentricities could be – and would be – overlooked. Besides, people reasoned, the Buttses were the only parents in this lowcountry town to have a son living in Hollywood and starring in blockbuster movies. For that, they would be permitted a measure of outlandishness.

THREE

DUE TO BRUISING ON HIS BRAIN, Guy eluded clear mindedness for several days. A thick rod and several pins were inserted to hold his leg together, while a morphine drip kept him temporarily unaware of the pain's intensity.

Guy slipped in and out of consciousness as nurses routinely fluttered about his room. Maddie hovered anxiously.

"You need to get out of here and rest," said Dr. Ledger, putting his hand on Maddie's shoulder and squeezing it. He rubbed at her neck. She looked up at him and gave him a tired smile. Her gaze returned immediately to Guy's face, covered in a mummy-like bandage.

"I'm going to have them bring a fold-out in here again," she said. "I don't go on until tomorrow. I'll rest until then. I want to be here in case he wakes up."

"Maddie ... you know that might not ... You know we did all that we could."

"I know that. I just think someone should be here ... in case. It's going to be difficult for him ... if he does ... you know, especially at first."

Dr. Ledger sighed. He waited and then composed his words. "According to you, this man hasn't given two shakes for you since he left here, Maddie. He ..."

"Stu ..." She was too tired to get into an argument with him. Her exhaustion almost caused her to snicker at his use of "two shakes." She typically admired him for always coming up with some clever way to avoid foul language, but this time she felt a slight giggle rising up in her. *I must be deliriously tired*, she thought. She contained herself.

"I just don't want to see you throw yourself into this ... into him. You'll make yourself ill ... and for what? He obviously didn't care too much about himself or anyone else – for that matter – or he wouldn't be in this shape."

"Not now, Stu," she said, still looking at Guy.

"Okay." Dr. Ledger leaned over and kissed her cheek. He squeezed her shoulder again. "Get some rest."

Maddie stared at Guy, remembering the first time *he* had kissed her. She was almost 12 and he was 11. Pretending to play Rhett Butler in *Gone With the Wind*, the movie that his parents made him watch at "least 999 times," he walked up to her assuredly, put his hand on the back of her head, gazed at her for a moment – while she furled her brow in confusion – and kissed her firmly on the lips. Maddie boxed him so hard on his right ear that he told her he had to ice it all night.

They had been telling one another ghost stories in his yard, sitting under the tree with the most bottles on display. The full moon illuminated the glass to reveal reedy branches inside that held the bottles in place. Guy and Maddie tried to outdo one another with horrific details to make the stories more gruesome with each telling. Maddie rose slowly from where they were sitting on the exposed roots at the base of the venerable oak. She was using hand gestures to embellish her version of the tale. Something about the way the bottles glowed and framed her made Guy rise and make his move.

He would not kiss her again until he was 15. That time she did not box him. By then she thought she wanted his touch, although she was still perplexed by her feelings for him. He was both fraternal and her best friend; she questioned whether she should have any physical feelings for him at all.   They were sitting and talking at Newnan's Marsh. His approach was abrupt, unanticipated. For the first time Maddie grasped, *felt*, the meaning of the word passion, which ignited in her like a match light; but that stirring was doused ever so quickly as simultaneous laughter erupted mid-kiss.

"What the hell!?"

"Don't say 'hell', Guy," scolded Maddie, "or that's where you might end up."

Then she laughed so hard that tears streamed down her face. "Oh, I have to pee!" she said, pushing him away from her.

"We must be havin' some of those ragin' hormones," yelled Guy after her as she disappeared behind some scrub trees.

They talked about being boyfriend and girlfriend after that, but decided against it.

"Naw, it's too weird," said Guy. "I love you, but you're Maddie. I can't go around saying you're my girlfriend. It's too whacked. Besides, that would greatly limit me from pursuing other girls," he said in a teasing British accent.

She recalled how he smiled flirtatiously at her. He was so handsome, his dark brown hair in a wavy mess. Green eyes. Smile that was always playful, toying with her, egging her on – daring her to dispute him. She could not stay mad at him, ever.

"But you're the only one I ever want to have sex with," she said suddenly.

"Sex! Maddie ... good grief. Where did that come from? Sex!"

"I mean when we're married, of course, Guy. We are going to get married one day, aren't we? I mean we can't just go off with someone else. We have to stay together, don't we?"

Maddie could still feel the long, throbbing silence that ensued.

She remembered, painfully, Guy's speech: "Maddie, you know I'm going to Hollywood. I've always talked about that. That's what my parents expect and that's what my dream is. I'm going to be a great actor! Maybe when I make it big, then you can come out to Hollywood and we can get married there. How about that? You said you wanted to be a doctor. Heck, there's lots of people in California who'll need a doctor."

They did not talk about sex or marriage or the future perimeters of their relationship anymore after that. Maddie promised herself she would not bring it up. The important thing, she decided, was that they were best friends and inseparable. Everyone at their school knew they were a team. Both only children, they were to one another the missing sibling, the adventurous playmate, the loving pest, and – always – a refuge when life bore down.

Maddie grew up, in fact, with Guy at her side exploring the salt marshes and creeks that surrounded Wynee. They knew each other in kindergarten and first grade, but it was not until the second grade that they connected. Maddie was actually almost a year older than Guy because she was born right after the school start cut-off date, but Guy always said that since she was such a "shrimp" no one knew she was any older.

On the playground one day, while Maddie was pretending pet store with Annalee – she was the white Persian kitten for sale and Annalee was the pet shop owner – Guy strutted over like a grownup, pretended to pull money out of his pocket and slap it down on the counter, and announced confidently: "I'll take that pretty little kitty right there. The one with the blue eyes."

Maddie smiled at this memory.

The next day before recess Guy asked if he could play pet shop with them. Annalee creased her forehead and did not acquiesce at first, but Maddie convinced her that to play it correctly, they really did need a customer.

After a while, Annalee's furrow became a frown; she bowed out – ungraciously. She told Maddie that the choice would have to be made between her and "that boy". Guy never whined, bossed her, or gave her an ultimatum, so Maddie picked him.

When they were in the fourth grade, they decided to meet after school and play. They worked it all out. He would go to her home one day, and she would go to his next. They only lived eight blocks away from each other. Maddie's home was a tidy historic Dutch Colonial on one end of the small town, while Guy's, with its disheveled ambiance and looming fluted columns, stood practically at the entrance to Wynee.

Maddie thought the only obstacle to Guy playing at her house would be Miss Sumney. It turned out she was right.

Maddie's father, Dr. Walker, was Wynee's pediatrician and pediatric surgeon. He worked. Always. In fact, Maddie rarely remembered him at home. Her mother died when she was a baby so Miss Sumney stepped in to help and was always there for Maddie until Dr. Walker came home. Often it was very late. Sometimes, when Maddie was too young to stay by herself, Dr. Walker asked Miss Sumney to spend the night. Miss Sumney's sister, also her next-door neighbor, kept an eye on her own children whenever she was called at night to care for Maddie. She seemed a constant presence to Maddie since her father was rarely around. Miss Sumney was her cook, comforter, healer, spiritual guide, and mental mender. And for a while, toddling and innocent, until she became old enough to ask the right questions, Maddie thought Miss Sumney was her mother – even though she was never allowed to call her "mommy" or "momma" like other kids called theirs.

"Are you my momma?" she blurted out one day when Miss Sumney was folding her daddy's underwear.

"Heavens no, child," she dismissed. "I'm as black as night and you're as white as day. How can I be your momma? You think that's normal, child? Mercy. You'll learn soon enough. That kinda thing ain't happenin' in Wynee. No way. No how."

"Then where's my momma? Do I have one?" asked Maddie.

"She died, child. She died when you was just a babe. She's in heaven now, child."

Squash Sumney tended to her, but no, she was not her momma. Dried her tears when she cried, but rarely had an enduring hug for her. Just did not have time, was what Maddie figured. Besides, she had her own boy and girl to take care of when she finished at the Walkers. Maddie thought Miss Sumney would fuss about her bringing a boy home to play with, but she was not quite prepared for how much.

"What you doin' here?" yelled Squash as Guy followed Maddie into the backyard of the Walker home.

"He …," started Maddie.

Guy grinned widely and exclaimed: "I came to play with Maddie, Miss Sumney. Ain't you Mater's sweet mama?"

"Yes sir. I am," she answered, squinting her eyes tight and straining in the sunlight to identify Maddie's cocky companion. "And what is your name, young man?"

"Why, it's Guy ... Guy Olivier Rhett Butts."

Maddie beamed at him. Surely his charms had already softened Miss Sumney's heart. She averted Miss Sumney's eyes. "Come on, Guy. Let's go swing!" She grabbed his hand and pulled him toward the metal swing set.

"Maddie Elaine Walker! Come here this instant!"

Maddie dropped Guy's hand. She slowly walked back toward the porch where Squash loomed.

"What that boy doin' here?"

"I'm playing with him Miss Sumney, ma'am."

"It ain't right for him to be here."

"Why not?"

"It just ain't, that's why not. You tell him to go on home," said Squash, making a gesture as if to shoo a fly.

"I want to know why it isn't right," Maddie stood, defiantly, as Squash faced her. "I play with Mater when he comes with you sometimes. He's a boy."

"That's different."

"How?"

" 'Cause it is. Lord, child." She sighed, exasperated. To Guy, who was swinging happily and watching the scene unfold, she yelled, "You go on home now! Maddie can't play right now!"

"No! He's my friend! He's my ... *best* friend!" Maddie protested. She decided right then that Miss Sumney, who was not her momma, would not tell her who she could play with.

"Well, child, you're goin' to have to make another new *best* friend. Your daddy's goin' to hear about this and you and Mr. Butts ain't goin' to be friends no more."

"It was fun, Maddie, but I'm going to head home now," called out Guy, who strolled – smiling – across her backyard. He was beaming and waving, unaffected by the conflict. Maddie was furious. When she was angry, she cried. That day she remembered stomping by Miss Sumney so loudly that she thought the old German cuckoo clock on the wall in the hallway would come off its hanger. Squash ignored her. Maddie would certainly bring it up with her daddy when he got home from work.

She was in her room with the door closed when he arrived home at 6:11, according to the radio clock beside her bed. He was rarely home for dinner; he often ate what Miss Sumney saved him at a late hour. Maddie waited for him to say goodnight to Miss Sumney before she went down to greet him. Dinner was warm and ready for them to eat. He looked tired. He always looked tired. And he was quiet. He always seemed a little sad to her. Maybe he still missed her mother. She never brought that up with him though. It was his unspoken request, something she sensed, that her mother not be a topic of conversation. Even when the curiosity rose up geyser-like in her, she controlled her tongue. Miss Sumney told her that someone named Apostle James wrote in the Bible about uncontrollable tongues setting forest fires ablaze. She did not know what that meant, but she did not want to be the cause.

She sat across from his elevated, angular frame and asked him how his day was. He said, "fine." She was inwardly grateful that he was actually home on time – on a night of such import. She devised that after Miss Sumney's always-satisfying meal, he would settle down into his ample coffee-finished leather, button-tufted club chair. That would be the time to approach. Predictably, he did sit in his chair, and she took no time snuggling up in his lap.

He was more solemn than usual, she observed. Before Maddie had a chance to air her grievances regarding Miss Sumney, her father spoke up: "Miss Sumney already told me what happened today, turtle." (He called her a different animal name whenever they talked. It was his way.) "Said you had a ... a Guy Butts over here to play with you?"

"Yes, Daddy, he's my best friend," she talked fast. "He's nice, and not like some of those whiney, bossy girls at school. He's fun. He said his daddy is the mayor-straight or something like that. Sounds important, so he's from a nice fa..."

"I know who he is," her father said, a bit too intensely.

Maddie felt his arms tighten around her, gripping. She stiffened.

"Daddy ..." she pleaded.

"You find some good girl friends to play with, lamb, and that's the last we'll talk about Mr. Butts. Do you understand?"

"No Daddy, I don't ..."

Maddie's father lifted her off his lap and led her, silently, to her bedroom. He put her in her bed, kissed her on the top of her head, and turned to leave her room.

"I don't understand, Daddy," said Maddie, close to tears. "I don't."

"We don't understand all things," answered Dr. Walker, closing her door. "Some things are best left alone."

"So you don't want me playing with Guy? Ever?" she asked.

He did not answer her. She listened to him pad soberly down the groaning staircase as if he were in a funeral procession, then she released the second wave of tears cried that day because of her friend Guy.

Maddie told Guy the next day that if they were playing after school, they would have to do it at his house. She did not tell him about what her father said to her the night before. But when Maddie scootered the sidewalks to Guy's house – after she had eaten a snack, finished her homework, and lied to Miss Sumney about going to play with some classmates at Centerpoint Park – she was met with another peculiar reaction from Guy's father.

"What did Guy say your name was?" asked Lawrence Butts, home resting after a late night case involving a domestic dispute that led to a traffic violation.

"Maddie, I mean Madeline ... Walker."

Guy's father drew in a deep breath and smiled insincerely.

"Oh," he said gravely, before turning and walking slowly back inside the house.

"Let's not play here either," said Guy, perplexed by his father's rudeness. That day they did go to Centerpoint Park, and Maddie was glad she did not really, when you got right down to it, lie to Miss Sumney.

The next day Guy told her, "My dad said I should play with boys my age and not girls, especially one almost a year older than I am. I'm not sure how he knew you were older. Oh well. I told him you were almost like a boy ... that you liked to do cool things. He was pretty stern about it though. Not sure why."

"Why are our dads acting all wacko about us being friends?" blurted out Maddie.

"Did your dad act wacko?" asked Guy.

"A little," she said. She wanted to say *a lot*, but she left it at a little.

"Beats me why. Well, anyway, we don't have to play at either of our houses. We've got all over town, plus all the salt marshes and the creeks to play in. Just as long as I'm home by suppertime is what the rule is at my house."

"Oh ... I'm, uh, sure I can do that, too," said Maddie. She was not really certain; in fact, she felt in her heart it was not likely, but she wanted to sound like everything would be fine.

She would figure out a way to play with her friend. She would offer to Miss Sumney that she *was* getting a bit older and could play responsibly away from home. Besides, the town was fairly small, with two main roads that ran parallel with the marsh waters, Front Street and Water Street, and one main square with a park and a gazebo. Then there were just a few shops, like Sweet Stuff Candies, a barber shop with the old-fashioned red, white, and blue barber pole out front, plus the public buildings, like the library and a tiny post office. Live oaks with outstretched branches and dangling tresses of Spanish moss hovered protectively over the wide, well-planned streets. Flower boxes in shop windows exuded calm and security. Other children her age roamed carefree within the confines of Wynee. She should be able to as well.

Maddie waited a few weeks so that Miss Sumney might forget about the whole "Guy thing" and then she sprang it on her that some friends were meeting at Newnan's Marsh to fish and play with marsh crabs after their snack and homework. "Yes," she would wear her black rubber boots and "Yes," she would be home way before dark.

Maddie grabbed a bucket and let the screened door slam hard, walking fast out of the yard before Miss Sumney had a chance to ask questions or think of a reason she should not go. Maddie meandered down a clear path made through reeds that clicked as the wind blew them together. At the mucky water's edge she met a friend, not friends. And they did fish and they did catch fiddler crabs, so she was not really lying about that. And if anyone caught them and asked where the other "friends" were, Maddie had decided she would say that they must have changed their minds. She even brought a little fiddler crab home that night as an "overnight guest" to prove her case without a doubt. All her father asked that evening was, "Did you have a good day?"

At first, Maddie's after-school adventures with Guy were mild. Increasingly, the two risked pressing beyond the cocoon of their benign community. Their afternoon jaunts through Newnan's Marsh sometimes meandered into the neighboring

Lorry's Marsh, crabs scattering like hundreds of panicked onlookers in every direction as they walked on vast mud flats. The long necks of snowy and great egrets peeked above the dense cord, spike, and black grasses covering most areas of the seemingly infinite marsh lands.

The marshes were so named, they had heard, because of the homesteads or plantations that once thrived there along the banks – when the waters grew rice and not just fiddler crabs and oysters. Those places were mostly gone. A few venerable structures held on, but Maddie's father told her that during the Civil War impressive homes were targets of Yankee torches. Charred remains of a home's footprint, long grasped and devoured by the earth, were commonplace in South Carolina – especially in the last months of the War when Sherman's men left reminders that secession had not been such a good idea.

Maddie and Guy learned to judge the tides. If the tide was particularly low and they felt like they could chance it, they would run the mud flats to the forest's edge and then pick their way among the pond pines and scrubby post oaks that grew sparsely along the shores. At the forest's borders looking back, Maddie imagined what a rice plantation owner must have felt like surveying the wide expanse of marsh grasses; depending on the season, it was an emerald or wheat horizon that stretched on and on.

"Hear the ocean!" Maddie would proclaim, looking out over the endless marsh grasses and beyond the Wyneealechee River that flowed – eventually – into the ocean about five miles away.

"It's the wind," dismissed Guy.

"I know it's the ocean," insisted Maddie. "Just listen. Can't you hear the waves?"

"What? You got bionic ears?" laughed Guy.

Maddie thumped one of Guy's ears. "No, smartie! I just think that's the ocean. That's all!"

The waterways running through the marsh grasses filled up and drained with the tides like a long breath. On sunny summer days at low tide, the plethora of green in the grasses ranged from muddy to brilliant. Some people in Wynee scheduled their days to the lows and highs of the tidal marshes, and Guy and Maddie were no exception. The two friends explored the wilderness of forest beyond marshes, but they knew they had to judge the tides in order to return home in time.

Their jaunts advanced beyond conformity. They explored the outer reaches of Wynee's protective arms. Once they found what became known to them as Duckweed Pond. They named it, but Guy found out inadvertently that it was covered in duckweed. *It warmed Maddie to think on it.* When they first came upon the sight, the smooth carpet of shimmering green, luminescent in the bright sun, was too much for Guy to resist. The borders of the area were dense with weeds and brush, except for one opening. At first glance, the pond beckoned as a curious oval disk lying green and still in the woods.

"Cool!" said Guy, moving toward the edge. "Looks like an alien's been here!" He was drawn, trance-like, to its shape and color; Maddie closely inspected the shape's edge.

"Guy, these are ..." But before the word "plants" escaped her lips, Guy had taken another step, onto, and into, a pond. The solid shape, which formed from thousands of small, flat water plants huddled together to create a mirage over the pond's surface, broke apart. Startled, Guy tripped and fell back into the water, further disrupting the pristine image.

"Oh man!" yelled Guy. "Man! What the …"

Maddie roared. "That's probably where the Swamp Thing lives! Or at least a giant alligator!"

"Ha. Ha. Very funny." Craven, he threw his wet body on the muddy shore and crawled a few yards away from the pond's edge. His jeans were covered in green specks.

"You look like you're turning into the Swamp Thing!" laughed Maddie, holding her side. "Oh ... Guy ... What's that saying, 'Look before you ...' step into something green!"

"It's before you 'leap'," he grimaced, standing up and stomping his feet, trying to shake the miniature lilypad-shaped plants from his legs. "And if you don't stop laughing and poking fun at me, I'll pick up your rear and throw you in there! You will get to find out real fast whether or not a hungry gator's hold up in there!"

That night Guy told his father about the pond. Even though his father was less adamant than Maddie's about them playing together, Guy left out the fact that only the two of them were exploring. Lawrence assumed, proudly, that his son's wilderness surveys involved other boys. His father further enlightened him about duckweed – but he also offered a warning about the area: "Near there, I've been told, is where that teenage girl and boy were found by some hunters, dead ... a knife wound to both their hearts. It happened a long time ago. Never did find the killer ... or the knife. Sadly, never determined their identities either. People around here say no one was looking for them. They're the ones buried in the town cemetery. Church folks at Bethel Methodist take turns caring for their sites."

The next day Maddie and Guy bee-lined it for the cemetery and studied the gravestones until they came upon one that read, "Male Unknown" and another beside it that read, "Female Unknown."

"I thought your daddy had to be pulling one over on you ... just to scare you from going back there again," said Maddie.

"Me too," said Guy.

"Those poor, poor people," said Maddie. "Their mommas and daddies must be wonderin' where they are."

"Let's go," said Guy, grabbing at the back of her shirt to get her attention. He began walking out of the cemetery.

"Where?" asked Maddie.

"I want to go explorin' around there some more. Maybe we'll be the ones to find the knife. We'll be local heroes."

"You'll do anything to get on television, Guy. No way, no how. Your daddy's scary story might not have worked on you, but it was enough for me."

Guy persisted; a few days later they headed back to their duckweed pond. It became a frequent excursion site, and nothing abysmal ever happened. No dead bodies. No criminals hiding out. No knives caked with old blood. But they did search for that knife. Heads down, they shuffled their feet among the pine needles and leaves, canvassing a wide area, until they heard about a hunter almost dying from a copperhead bite; the camouflaged serpent the color of leaves and pine straw.

They ventured farther one day, along what seemed to be an abandoned road. Guy was determined to learn where the road led. On either side of the road were woods, their flooring thick with a spongy accumulation of pine needles and leaves discarded by the endless cycle of seasons. Dwarf palmettos dotted the woods along the dirt roadside – half circles of green against the grays and browns of the forest. Spontaneously, Guy detoured and ripped off a few of the palm's fronds. He tossed one to Maddie and challenged her to a dual. They pretended to fence under the canopy of trees shading the road. Guy lunged in for a real poke.

"Ouch! Guy!" said Maddie.

"Sorry! I didn't mean to really stick you." He turned around, smirking, pretending to strut off victoriously.

Maddie raced up behind him and stuck him in the back, the frond's pointy end entering the shirt's fabric. Guy howled.

"Hey! Foul play! Foul play!" said Guy, rubbing the sting at his lower back.

"Sorry," said Maddie smiling.

They both agreed to throw down their flimsy green weapons. After a few minutes more of walking, the road widened and two straight lines of enormous live oaks – a multitude of outstretched twisted arms reaching toward earth or sky – lined the roadway. The limbs of the oaks overlapped in the middle of the road and formed a natural, tangled arch.

"Wow! This had to be where a plantation once was," said Maddie.

"Yeah. It looks like we're going to walk right up on Tara," said Guy.

They ambled a short distance farther and stopped suddenly. Before them was the decaying shell of a once-glorious mansion. A precise square-shaped granite foundation was obvious; four lofty circular brick columns indicated the home's front and back entrances. The back of the grand estate, they surmised, must have once faced the marsh or been accessible by a creek, but layers of overgrowth obscured factual evidence of their theory. Another oak – a looming sentry larger than the ones lining the drive – guarded the main yard. Its limbs, once kept under control with careful pruning, stretched and strayed over the architectural ruins to provide an awning heavy with Spanish moss.

"Cool!" said Guy simply. "Way cool. Do you think anyone knows about this place?"

"They have to know about it," said Maddie smartly. "There probably was once a main road to it. It's just been forgotten."

"Well, it's ours now!" said Guy proudly. "This is our new hangout!"

And then, in true "Guy style" – what drew Maddie to him on the playground in elementary school and what would detach him from her years later – he pompously ascended remnants of a wide marble stairway, turned theatrically, stood as if he were holding up the columns with his might, and boomed a Charlton Heston imitation, "I am Moses! I come to free my people! Come, Zipporah, and be by my side as we petition the Pharaoh to let my people go!"

That day, Guy melded into the character of Moses. Maddie became his Zipporah ("Zipp," for short), and it stuck. On some occasions, he pleaded, until she relented, to act with him, but she was never any good. He dominated all the lines anyway. She just had to stand there in that grand place and look admiringly at him.

The second time they visited the relic, which Guy dubbed their "promised land," he made his speech in Pharaoh's "temple," and then ran and climbed easily to an area of the dignified oak that made a sort of platform of two wide limbs closely spaced. He stood, erect, balancing on a vertical limb, pretending to survey a vast land in the distance. "There, my people," he said pointing, "is the land of milk and honey."

Maddie climbed the tree after him, laughing. "Whatcha' laughin' at 'Zipp'? Don't laugh at your Moses now! He might have to turn you into a camel with his holy staff!"

They sat together in that imposing tree and giggled and marveled about finding such a remarkable place. They rested against the limbs, covered in soft moss, and contemplated the moss hanging over their heads.

"When I'm a rich movie star, I'm going to come back here and buy this place and fix it up!" said Guy. Then, "You can live here with me and tend to our gardens, Zipp!"

Maddie smiled. He was always dreaming. They were not long in the tree when Guy looked at his watch. They could never dally in their promised land, or anywhere else for that matter, for the impending tides always drove them home. They had to scurry, leaving their palatial hideaway behind, to avoid being hemmed in by the marsh. As it was, they sometimes had to wade in water up to their knees to reach Wynee's shores before the marshes swelled again.

Bites from miniscule red chigger bugs that live in tree moss covered Maddie from head to toe the next day. The friends were absent from school the better part of a week, tortured by the irritation and itching of the bugs, which burrow into the skin and can only be suffocated and killed by what Miss Sumney called the "nail 'em" treatment: tiny drops of clear nail polish on each bite. "The polish closes that airway off to the critter," she explained to Maddie. "Can't breathe. So they die."

Miss Sumney poked at Maddie, adding to her agony. "I 'magine you look like a leper, from the Bible. Lordy, girl, what were you doin' in a tree anyways? Thems for boys to climb. By the ways," she looked at her crossly, "I hear talk at Lollie's that Mr. Butts's son, Guy, 'member him? Hmmm? Well, he's got the chigger bites too. Wouldn't be up in a tree with that boy now, would ya?

"No, ma'am," she lied deftly.

Occasionally, Maddie and Guy were accompanied, ironically enough, by Mater, Miss Sumney's son, who was one year older than Maddie; he was an apt fisherman and brought along his cane pole. Keen with lofty ambitions, Maddie remembered Mater as always wanting to "get outta here" when he graduated high school. And Maddie's next door neighbor, Gracie, shy and with few friends, came along sometimes as well – mostly to give Maddie more validity. Maddie strolled, arm in arm, with Gracie down the sidewalk right in front of

Miss Sumney as if to say, "See here, we're hanging out togeth-er ... us girls ... no boys involved."

Of course, Guy and Maddie required Mater and Gracie to swear, on the threat of pain and immense suffering and the lives of their future children, that the day's report to parents would leave out the fact that Guy was present when Maddie was there or vice versa. Mater and Gracie did not understand what the big deal was about, but they agreed to the condi-tions. As far as Guy and Maddie knew, they stayed true to their word. They revealed some of their discoveries to Mater and Gracie; the mansion, though, was theirs alone.

At the dinner table some nights, it was Guy who slipped and said "Maddie" now and then. His father shot him a look and his mother would say, "Who is that, dear?" He quickly responded casually, "Just some girl at school." He slipped and mentioned her name way too often, he decided, but he never actually said that he played exclusively with her after school. He did not know what the stress was about anyway. But Maddie demanded secrecy. And he felt intuitively that it was not in their best interest to be out in the open with his parents or anyone else for that matter. Her father and Miss Sumney's reactions to Guy put her on edge. She did not want Guy revealing to his parents that they were playing together so often. It was a small town; his parents could easily talk to her dad about it. They were both a little surprised someone in the town had not yet poked a nose into the whole situation. Guy told her it was all so confusing.

"I know," she cajoled, "but if we aren't careful, we won't be able to play together anymore. I don't know why, but we just won't."

Then Maddie remembered being shocked silly when Guy said to her at school first thing one Monday morning: "Boy, have I got something to tell you!"

He tried to tell her at lunch, but Freddie Sanders and Butch McGraw decided to brag to Guy about all the excruciating and bloody details of their weekend deer hunting trip with their dads. Of course, Guy could not tell them he was not interested and wanted instead to talk to a girl. He just shot her an "Oh well" look across the cafeteria tables. She was crazy to know. She passed him a note in history class: *Please tell me!* And they almost got caught when he passed her the note back: *I will after class! Patience, Zipp!*

After school, Guy was nowhere to be found. They were supposed to meet at the Feed and Seed after snack and home-work to buy new $3.99 black rubber boots for marsh wading. But she was hoping to catch him before that.

She hurried through snack and homework while Miss Sumney looked on. "Lord child, you're goin' to choke your-self. Where you goin' in such a hurry?"

"Marsh explorin'," managed Maddie with a mouth full of an Oreo.

"Well, that ain't no reason to make yourself sick over. The marsh ain't goin' nowheres. You slow down, you hear?"

Maddie did not. She stuffed, swallowed, and hurried out the door to meet Guy. He was a few minutes late. "What took you so long?" she asked him, but impatiently prodded: "Never mind that, what is it you want to tell me?"

Beauford Johnson was standing at the doorway of his Feed and Seed store. "Hi, kiddos! You musta' outgrown or outworn your boots again. You come right on in here, and I'll fix you up."

Maddie sighed. She knew she would have to wait even lon-ger for the information. When they were outside the confines of Wynee's auditors, with the marsh's boggy slime merging with the blackness of their new boots, Maddie demanded, "Okay, spill it!"

"It's been about to kill you, hasn't it?" teased Guy.

"Just spill it or I'll bean you with a pluffmud ball!"

Some days during low tide in their playground of wet plains, they had pluff mud wars, a game they invented. They rolled dozens of tiny balls out of the sticky, clay-like substance and filled individual buckets. Too much ammunition and the bucket was cumbersome to carry back to the woods, where they used the trees as shields. Each direct hit, which left a small brown mark on their body or clothes, was a point. Much to Miss Sumney's chagrin, Maddie would often be covered with drying brown spots when she arrived home after a pluff mud war. Guy was a much better aim. "Are you a girl or wild Indian," Miss Sumney would huff. "You need to sit your back-side down in your room and play with dolls and girly stuff and stop runnin' wild. People be thinkin' your daddy ain't raisin' you right."

Standing erect as if preparing for the performance of his life, Guy announced what Maddie was dying to hear: "This is how it happened … It was right after church, and my parents called me into the library. They were sitting there holding hands and being all lovey dovey and stuff." He made a sour face.

"I figured they musta' just watched a love story the night before ... one of them romances, and they wanted to teach me some message in it or something. Yuck and double yuck! Anyway, Daddy says, 'Guy, I need to ask your forgiveness for something. God showed me today in church that my heart hasn't been right about something.' I wanted to tell him that I was in that same church and I didn't actually see God show-ing anybody anything, but I didn't. I just listened. He said, and get this, 'We had an *adult issue* with the Walkers years ago and that's why I acted a little strangely when you brought Madeline home to play with you that first day. I really didn't want you playing with Madeline because of unforgiveness and a feeling of guilt in my own heart. I spoke to your mother, and she feels the same way.'"

Maddie recalled an inability to respond. She had stared at him wide-eyed for silent seconds. "What in the world?" she finally responded.

Of course, she learned in later years what he was talking about. But she certainly had no clue then.

"Yeah, they said all that," attested Guy. "I have *no idea* what they were talking about. I asked him, 'What kind of adult issue?' but he just told me that's why it's called an adult issue – 'cause it's the business of adults. He said for me not to worry myself about it, that it was over and done and that God wanted everyone to forgive one another and that he knew I really wanted to be friends with you because I talked about you sometimes. He said he also knew I was playing with you in the afternoons. 'Parents aren't as dumb as you think,' he said. My mom was just sitting there holding his hand and nodding her head 'yes' the whole time he was talking. Then, *and here's the topper* …"

Maddie leaned into him, listening intently.

"Daddy said, 'We think God wants us to call Dr. Walker and invite him and his girl to church with us on Sunday. We think that if you and Maddie want to be friends, it should be in the presence of God."

"Oh no," said Maddie, "No … Oh …" She felt like she had just taken a line-drive softball to her gut. "They can't do that! My daddy will be beside himself if he knows I've been hangin' out with you all this time after school. I'll be killed! Miss Sumney will slaughter me! Definitely on restriction forever! They can't do that, Guy. Besides, my daddy doesn't go to church. He might be offended if they even ask him. And the only time I've been to church is on Christmas to that black church with Miss Sumney. Oh no, Guy. They can't. No way."

"Way," said Guy, matter-of-factly.

"What do you mean?" said Maddie, feeling angry and nauseous at the same time. She was standing ankle deep in the mire.

"My daddy called your daddy late last night. I stayed up and tried to listen. I think your daddy hung up on mine at first, but my daddy just persisted and called him back. All I could hear were some of his words: 'forgiveness … God … don't be mad at her … they're innocent kids … I'm sorry.' He said 'I'm sorry' a bunch. I just wonder what coulda' happened."

Maddie realized that she had already gone to sleep before her father had gotten home that evening. He called her from the hospital earlier to say that he was checking on a little boy with a dangerous case of the flu. "Night, chicken," he had said to her. In the morning, he had already left for work.

"Oh … gosh … Guy," she felt she would heave onto the marsh bottom. "I can't even think about going home now. I can't *believe* your father did that!"

"'Just trust in God and lean not on your own understanding,' is what Daddy told me this morning. He said that the conversation with your daddy went fine and that he *might* let you go to church on Sunday with us. He said he would think about it."

"So he wasn't *super* mad?" asked Maddie, feeling her stomach suddenly settle a bit.

"Didn't sound like it. But you know how parents are always trying to grease things over," said Guy.

"Oh thanks, Guy. That makes me feel better." She tromped out of the marsh. "I'll see you later."

"Where are you goin'?"

"Home!" she yelled. "I have to get myself all prepared for my daddy comin' home tonight. If you don't see me again because I'm dead or locked in my room for the rest of my life, it's been nice known' ya."

Maddie remembered fretting profusely that afternoon. Her father and Miss Sumney would never forgive her, and they would never trust her again; she was certain of that.

Early that evening, Maddie volunteered to help Miss Sumney peel shrimp and slice tomatoes for supper. They were well into August, but the lingering sear kept South Carolinians into tomatoes sometimes beyond the piles of browning leaves. Squash was preparing shrimp and grits, a recipe uniquely hers due to the bits of fresh tomatoes and locally cured ham she mixed in. Out of all the wonderful dishes she concocted in that kitchen, it was Dr. Walker's favorite. Maddie cherished it as well, though an appetite escaped her that particular evening.

"Lord, child. You musta' done somethin' pretty bad!" said Miss Sumney bluntly while extracting sourdough bread from the oven.

"What do you mean?" asked Maddie, almost slicing into her finger. Panic flushed her face.

"You don't usually help me unless I threaten every hair on your head, and you haven't stopped askin' what you can do for me since you got home!"

"Well, fine then," said Maddie indignantly. She snapped her knife down on the cutting board and huffed upstairs to her room; her words trailed behind her: "If you don't need the help, then I've got plenty else to do!"

Maddie waited in her room until her father came home. *5:30.* She could not remember any time he had arrived home so early. She thought about going to meet him, but she lingered in her room.

Sure enough, he was home early to confront her. He entered her room. Cross-legged on the middle of her bed, she braced herself. Even though he was rarely at home, he was at all times a warm and affectionate father, slow to discipline. This night, however, he did not approach her amiably. No silly pet names. Instead of boiling over in anger and disappointment, he seemed heavy laden with a wretchedness unfamiliar to her. Redness rimmed his eyes. *Had he been crying?* He seated himself methodically onto her bed, his back slanted slightly away. He did not look at her directly.

He began: "I understand that, despite my objection, you have become close friends with Guy Butts … that you have, indeed, been friends with him for a while now. You have been playing with him after school."

"I'm sorry, Daddy."

He sat silently, searching. His anguish agonized her. She felt a horrible foreboding about defying him – about what he would reveal to her.

"I didn't really give you a reason why you shouldn't play with Mr. Butts, and really … there isn't a reason that is easy for me to explain. His father … parents … they, well, we just …"

"Did you have an argument?"

"Something like that," he said resignedly, not looking at her. "It was a long time ago. This is a small town. It's my fault. If I wanted you to stay away from them, I should have moved. It's just that I'm needed here, and …" He trailed off.

Maddie failed to follow him.

"If you want to be friends with Guy and friends with the Buttses … if you want to go to church with them, then go. You're alone so much, and I'm sorry for that. I'm sorry that you don't have your mother here to …"

Maddie's bed shuddered for an instant as her father, the strong, reliable town healer, tried to contain a sob. He rose precipitously from her bed and exited her room. She sat, stunned. And then the tears came. She sobbed into her pillow until she heard Miss Sumney's footsteps on the stairs. She tried to make it to the door in time to lock it. She did not want to deal with her reproach. Miss Sumney entered with a force that belied her petite form.

"Lord, child. You been cryin'? It's okay now, you come here to Miss Sumney."

In a rare demonstrative display, she embraced Maddie with thin arms and pulled her firmly against a flat bosom in the same way she had when Maddie, as a toddler, scraped her knees learning to walk, or when she suffered a splinter from the wooden sandbox. Even though Squash's slight frame offered little sanctuary, Maddie was fairly comforted. Yet, her shame at disappointing her father was afforded no real peace. A harsh reprimand, not empathy, is what had been the excruciating expectation.

"It's a wonder this stuff didn't come crashin' down on this house way before now," said Squash.

"Stuff?" managed Maddie, sniffling against Miss Sumney's bony chest.

"The sad stuff your Daddy's been carryin' around. Ain't that what you been talkin' about, child? The reason why he don't want nothin' to do with the Butts family? It's about time everyone just let it go. It's been long enough, and everyone have to live together in this pea-ninny little town."

"Let *what* go?" said Maddie, her wet eyes staring up at Squash.

"Oh child, you just stop worrin' yourself," said Miss Sumney, dismissingly. You be friends with the Buttses and just go on about your business. It's workin' itself out. The good Lord's helpin' with that now. Why He's even gettin' you into a church. Isn't that somethin'? Your daddy'll be fine. You'll be fine. It'll all work out just like the good Lord's plannin'. Now you wash your face. We got supper goin' on the table in five."

How did she know about it all? What happened? wondered Maddie.

A few minutes later, dry-eyed but red faced and puffy-eyed, Maddie met her father on the landing. He seemed to have collected himself, stoic. She grabbed his hand and said, "I love you, Daddy. I'm sorry for not being honest with you."

"I love you too, kitten."

What could have happened between her father and the Buttses maddened her for a few weeks. Whenever she was with Guy she speculated aloud every imaginable scenario her young mind could conjure. Guy told her not to worry about it. "Hey, we get to hang out without sneaking around," he reminded her. "And, you get to come to church and youth group with me now. It'll be fun!"

Gradually, it became one of those nagging thoughts that surfaced like a geyser when she was bored, disheartened, or – later – hormonal. But the family web remained guarded, while Guy and Maddie experienced freedom in a friendship that flourished. Unexpectedly, for Maddie, the liberty of their relationship was about more than just fun. Attending First Baptist of Wynee, listening to the preacher expound on such topics as talking angels and Jesus healing with mud – these were the things Miss Sumney carried on about sometimes, but not with any depth or real explanation. Maddie became transfixed. She asked Miss Sumney for a Bible for her birthday and, with an appetite like an animal out of hibernation, hungered for comprehension in the words. With gradual understanding, she began to feel a remarkable presence: a comforting love enveloping her in a sheltering blanket.

"You're becoming a better Christian than I am," remarked Guy, who sat next to her each Sunday during the service. He called her Zipp more often and teased her by dancing around her singing "Zippity Do Da" from the Disney animated Brer Rabbit movie.

Maddie felt awkward around the Buttses at first. The feeling seemed mutual. Initially, Charlene's shoulders stiffened and she clasped tightly her hands in front of her. Maddie observed that Lawrence noticed this too, and moved in to distract Charlene with an affectionate word or a diffusing rub on her back. Maddie studied them, and wondered. Increasingly, time birthed a closeness between them.

Guy's mother exhibited signs of peculiarity now and then, certainly. Most noticeably, she made the sign of the cross frequently, even though they were not Catholic. She blessed the car before they got into it. Each Sunday morning on their way to church she made the sign when they passed a plastic cross adorned with faded artificial flowers (most likely a memorial to a lost life in a car accident, Maddie ascertained). Charlene always crossed herself after every blessing. Baptists looked sideways at this gesture, but they let it slide. She was, after all, a Yankee. Wyneeans generally thought all Yankees were Catholic; they let it slide thinking it was as harmless as her Northern accent. Guy's life was immeasurably more interesting than hers. To have parents who watched movies all the time and took you to worship: *What could be better?*

On Sunday mornings, she bounded out of bed, exuberant to learn more about Him, have lunch not of pimento cheese sandwiches but northern favorites like peppered beef stew and shoofly pie – and to be blessed by Mr. Butts's kind words of thankfulness for the food, for everything. Sometimes Lawrence read from the book that he beheld second to the Bible: *Mere Christianity* by C.S. Lewis. When she turned 16, Maddie was given a copy of the book with these words by Lewis inscribed on the title page: "… forgive the inexcusable because God has forgiven the inexcusable in you". Following was scribbled: "You are loved! Guy, Charlene, Lawrence". She cherished it.

Talk was lively, a little quirky, certainly more interesting than conversations with her father. Guy seemed at ease with the whole picture. She cherished the Buttses for confronting her father. She forgave them for the unknown long before she knew. They taught her about faith. *Where would she be without it now?*

Although her vanilla childhood was enriched with layers of mint chip and rocky road when Charlene and Lawrence entered in, she did not let on around her father. Intuitively, she downplayed the lushness of her experiences with them. She loved her father and she felt a hurt emanating, so she stayed quiet.

The last time Guy kissed Maddie was when they were 18 and she was packing for USC. He bounded up the stairs and burst into her bedroom, "Hollywood, here I come!"

"God help Hollywood," said Maddie, sullenly.

Reflecting on this by Guy's bedside under the intensity of hospital lighting, she remembered foreboding heaviness – sadness bearing down. Guy's lightheartedness had exasperated her that day.

"Whatcha mopin' for," Guy had said, plopping down on her bed. "Aren't you excited? We're gettin' out of Wynee for a while. Nothin' but pure adventure waitin' for us."

"You aren't going to be able to say mopin', gettin', and waitin' when you get to Hollywood," she answered smartly. "You have to actually enunciate a 'g' sound on the end of those words, or they'll stick your hind-end right back on that plane heading south. Or, they'll cast you in some sort of Beverly Hillbillies remake movie and make fun of you."

"Well, I'm gettin' ... getting ... a speech coach when I get out there, Miss. You know, if you make it as a big shot doctor, you'll need to clean up your speech a little too. So, are you not excited about going to *USC*?"

"I'm excited," she answered, halfheartedly. She would not look at him. She continued to stuff jeans and t-shirts into her suitcase. If she saw a twinkle in those green eyes of his, she would box him for sure.

"It just came to me last night what my last name might be when I get to Hollywood," he said merrily. "That is, if it's not already taken. It just came to me all of a sudden. I wasn't even thinking about it. *Jamison*. Doesn't that go great with Guy? Real sophisticated. Has a nice ring to it. Guy Jamison. Sounds like a movie star, don't you think? Jamison. What do you think about that?"

Maddie slowly pulled underwear out of her dresser drawer. She kept her back to him. To halt tears, she bit her lower lip so hard a salty taste rose to her consciousness. She touched her lip and examined the spot of blood. She stayed turned, clutching the underwear; when she did not answer him, he continued to rattle on about Hollywood and his new name. No matter what, she did not want him to see her cry. She swallowed and tried to take a deep breath, to find her voice, but it was not there. She could not answer him.

"Maddie?"

She stayed turned from him.

"Maddie? Hey, what's up?"

He went to her then and tried to turn her toward him.

"Maddie." He wrapped his arms around her back.

The tears trickled … then flowed.

"Maddie ... I love you, you know that. We knew this day would come. Ever since we became buds, we knew this day would come. Nothing will change between us. You're my best ... *everything*. I love you, Maddie."

He turned her toward him and pulled a tissue out of the Kleenex box on the dresser. He dabbed at her tears and at the spot of blood on her lip.

Then he kissed her – not like the little pecks and flippant kisses he had given her at different times throughout their adolescence, and nothing even close to the time when their kiss had evoked a fit of laughter. A vine that began growing on that elementary school playground stole down and bound Maddie's soul. After he kissed her, he held her face delicately, then hugged her securely before telling her once more that he loved her and that he *would* stay in touch. They would always *be*, he had said. *Always*.

That kiss lingered for days ... months. *It was still there*. Looking at him in the hospital bed, his depleted, bruised, struggling body, she still felt the emotions that kiss had evoked.

He *had* forgotten her after he became a star. Quickly and mercilessly. Yet, Guy would forever inhabit his own private room in her soul.

FOUR

GUY RECOGNIZED THE VOICE. Familiarity. Distance.

He fought to comprehend his role. He could not remember the script. Obviously it was a hospital scene. He heard the sound of carts rolling down the hall; the constant beep-beep-beep of some kind of monitor. They made it all seem real, that was for certain. *It's not hard to get into character. But why can't I open my eyes?* The fog began to dissipate; comprehension steadily made its way. *That must have been some binger last night.* His clouded mind considered some sort of rubber mask constricting his senses, like the built and layered kind that took hours to construct for a scene often lasting only minutes. When he played in the film version of "Beauty and the Beast" he had to sit in a chair day in and day out while the makeup artists layered on rubberized prosthetics and added hair and makeup. They fussed at him when he tried to speak. It was maddening.

But now he could not speak. No matter how hard he tried to open his eyes or to move his lips, he could not.

This is some mask, he thought. He heard a groan. *His own?*

"Guy …"

He felt a warm hand atop his. *Maddie?*

Why is she in this movie? What is she doing here?
Some dream … drugs? Last night …

A rush of heat flooded his veins. Like water released from a dike, the sensation raced from his arm, up into his chest, across his midsection, and then settled into his bladder. He had an overwhelming need to relieve himself; it quickly dissolved and his body melded into the bed beneath him. He thought no more of acting, of anything.

Guy's every fiber and muscle threads guiding bones yearned acting. It was innate, his DNA, a natural instinct, his first memories. There was no beginning for him that did not involve movies, actors, or Hollywood. The Bible may have raised him up, but acting shaped his frame.

Certainly God's words were still there – dripped in through prayer and preaching from the minute he breathed his first until he bowed his head with parents and pastor at the air-port. He mostly recalled words when he thought of a wide-spread marsh at low tide; Psalm 23 sprang forth as naturally as his breath: "He makes me lie down in green pastures. He leads me beside still waters. He restores my soul." The words were there, a pleasant whisper from a friend. When he left Wynee, they remained; he just paid them no mind. Occasion-ally, while filming a scene, words pushed through the sludge and found their way to form on his lips, but Guy restrained them with scripted lines. He might consider what brought them there, for a second, and then dismiss the thought. He was an actor; no room for God in Hollywood. Better to leave Him in Wynee.

Guy was four when he flawlessly portrayed the Scarecrow in a shortened version of *Wizard of Oz*. His parents had applauded furiously; he knew then he would spend his life laboring on the craft. Yet, his need for the admiration he found in acting would often lead him into temptation, and down surreal and dangerous paths.

In some corners of Wynee, the term "modern" was unknown and irrelevant. When Guy and Maddie were not cavorting in the marshes to the east of Wynee, they were in the section of town referred to by Wynee's white population as Browntown. After Maddie's father acquiesced to her friendship with Guy, Maddie could visit the community without raising much of an eyebrow because Miss Squash Sumney, her son Mater, and her daughter Patience, resided here, as did many of Wynee's black residents. This land was set aside for African Americans after *the* war – one elongated strip of earth with fields on one side, woods on the other, and access to the creek at the end. The wide road down the middle was paved, though in disrepair. For nearly 100 years the road had been just dirt, with potholes so deep children used them as their private pools after a summer rainstorm.

If Maddie ever gave it a thought, she did not say anything to him, but Guy always considered how they were exiting one world and entering another as soon as they took their first steps onto Wallace Creek Road – named for the old Wallace family who once owned Browntown's land and then some. Those who resided in the neighborhood simply called it Our Road. Browntown was an obvious insult, and Wallace Creek Road reminded them that their ancestors once had a master whose name was immortalized in the official name of their street.

Contorted bicycles with peeling paint lined the road and littered many of the yards. The shotgun, clapboard houses, some in disrepair and patched with sheets of tin or exposed plywood, each had decent-sized covered front porches filled with well-worn La-Z-Boys, plastic lawn chairs, or rockers. A few homes stood brazenly painted a robin's egg blue or bright mustard, among other bold hues, but most were white washed, with paint visibly peeling or fading. Landscaping during summer months was a collection of 10-gallon buckets or white-painted tires serving as planters heavy with the weight of a favorite fruit: plump tomatoes.

At several homes, at least one resident occupied the front porch – or a spot under a shade tree. Children, sometimes three at a time, hung by armpits from tire swings. Mongrel bitches heavy with milk-filled teats, lounged around dark feet while their flea-infested mates scuffled in grassless yards. Initially, older residents might strain necks to peer at white intruders invading their domain; then they would settle back down, wave or shout a "how ya' doin'?" to the familiar forms of Guy and Maddie as they strolled carelessly down the middle of Wallace Creek Road.

Their goal was to get to the creek and the shrimp dock. Three Browntown brothers owned the Sock-'Em-Dog shrimp business; they pulled up hundreds of pounds of shrimp onto the decks of their trawlers during the week and then spent their Saturday mornings in a shack close to downtown selling the succulent crustaceans by the pound, raw or cooked up. Wyneeans lined up by the dozens to purchase ample takeout orders of the brothers' special-recipe, lightly battered and seasoned shrimp for Saturday dinners and Sunday brunches.

Only two of their trawlers were operational, and the brothers took them out mostly during spring and into late summer – May or June for the roe shrimp and June through August for brown shrimp. The white shrimp season geared up in the fall, beginning in August, peaking in September and October, and then typically tapering in December. The brothers stayed out, sometimes for a few days, searching for the active shrimp, whose daily routes are determined by tides.

Left behind at the dock was an eerie necropolis of half sunken ancient vessels, their masts struggling to stay above water. Some stood upright, but their masts hung with tattered rags and their hulls were rotting shells. Discarded and broken cables, used for hoisting the nets in and out of the water, littered the bases of the boats. An American flag at the top of one of the masts had deteriorated into a handful of stars and one shredded stripe. No one bothered to remove the spent ships, which suited Guy just fine. He knew the vessels would someday just disappear and become part of the creek. But he figured it would not happen anytime soon, or maybe not in his lifetime, so he enchanted himself by visiting the site as often as possible.

Guy and Maddie always approached the dock cautiously. They were certain the brothers would run them off if they caught them at the dock. "No Trespassing," posted predominantly at the entrance to the dock, was their telltale sign. All the times they dared trespass, though, the brothers were out shrimping. Guy never wanted to make any mischief or cause harm to the Sock-'Em-Dog business; he just wanted to board those old shrimp boats.

The pungent smell of discarded crustaceans overwhelmed them, but it made for a more authentic environment for play-acting.

"Come on, Maddie," he said, walking gingerly out to the most deteriorated end of the dock, its boards loose, broken, or missing along the way. "Your captain says you mates better board the ship and swab the decks."

Maddie roll her eyes.

"I'll make ye walk the plank for that one, missy."

They boarded Guy's favorite ship in the decrepit fleet. Barely visible on its side in faded white was the word "Duespaid." Guy thought it the most unusual, and yet fascinating, name for a ship. It sounded to him like the name of a ruffian pirate and he vowed to find out where the name originated. He chanted it in his head, "Duespaid," "Duespaid," "Duespaid." It wasn't until he was older and felt like a fool that he learned the weightiness of the words. He would come to physically understand their meaning.

Maddie complied grudgingly with Guy's need to entertain; while *in character* the two moved about the creaking, but still stable, hull, examining its abandoned and splintered remains.

"Fix the men a mess of those shrimp and make it snappy!" growled Guy. "There will be mutiny if these men get hungry. And besides, they need to have full bellies if we're goin' lootin' in the morn." Guy walked about the ship as if he had just one leg. Each time he spoke he puffed out his chest and set his jaw.

Maddie giggled.

"That, girl, has earned you time in the brig tonight!"

"Oh, no sir, Mr. Pirate, plleeeeasse, no," pleaded Maddie in a high-pitched, squeaky voice. "Not with the rats! Have mercy on my soul, sir!" She fell to her knees and clapped her hands together in prayer.

Guy just stood staring over her for a moment. Maddie pretended to cry in heaving, obnoxious sobs. It was times like these that he adored her friendship ... for yielding to his silly notions of play-acting. "Okay, okay. You're off the hook," he said, laughing and dismissing her with a sweep of his hand. "Let's look around here for that treasure map."

Guy began poking around in the rotten crevices of the shrimp boat.

"I've had enough of pirating on the high seas, Guy," said Maddie, after some time had passed. "It's about time to get home anyway."

"Just a minute. I just want to look around for another sec," he said.

His footsteps caused the boards beneath him to groan.

"Don't go way back there," warned Maddie. "The floor may cave in."

His eyes lit on something in a tight corner chink. Barely protruding from behind a cracked section of rotting wood was a shining piece of metal. "Maddie, come here. What's this?"

He gingerly pulled at a sharp point until it was free from the wood.

"What is it, Guy?" asked Maddie, keeping her position near the hull's exit.

Guy turned his back to her, fumbled for a moment with the metal object, and then turned quickly, a curved hook protruding from his pointer and middle fingers.

"Aye. Aye. It's Captain Hook to ye, missy! You'll be cookin' up me vittles tonight," he said, pointing the hook in Maddie's direction, "then swabbin' the deck thereafter."

Booming footsteps startled them both. They were heavy against the creaking boards of the old dock. They came quickly in their direction. Guy dropped the hook, which made a clanging sound against a section of old chain in disarray on the floor.

"Guy!" whispered Maddie intensely.

Guy grabbed her hand to pull her away from the hull's entrance and farther into the darkness when a shotgun barrel was thrust into the hull, almost knocking Maddie in the head. Behind it entered its carrier, Blizzard Sims, who dropped down like a heavy anchor. Both Guy and Maddie knew about Mr. Sims. Guy had heard his parents talk about his blackness and his height as if he were a Goliath-like figure, instead of a real person. Until that moment, they had not had the opportunity to experience his towering darkness up close. Blizzard had to bend, almost in half, to enter the hull. He pointed the shotgun at a shuddering Guy, who instinctively stepped in front of Maddie. Blizzard bellowed, "You ... don't ... belong here! Can't you read? It says, 'No Trespassing.' And that ain't an invitation. It means *no settin' foot* on this here boat or anywhere around in here. You got it?"

In his nervousness, Guy stifled a laugh at the thought that a man the color of tar could have acquired a name like Blizzard. Guy drove mirth from his mind and stared in awe at the threatening body filling the hull. Maddie peeked from behind Guy and spoke: "We understand, sir. We're sorry. This is just a really neat boat and ... uh ... we were just pretending to be pirates. We'll leave now. Sorry, sir. It won't *ever* happen again. Right, Guy?"

"Uh … right, sir. Sorry sir. We will go now."

Maddie took a step forward, hoping Mr. Sims would step aside and let them out. But he stayed and stared at the children. A wily grin formed at the corners of his mouth.

"Pirates? Playin' pirates, huh? Well, I reckon' this here offense could be forgotten and parents not be told or the police not called if you pirates will do some deck swabbin' for me. Get on out here!"

Guy looked confusedly at Maddie. Maddie shot him an angry glance. They followed Blizzard and his shotgun out of the hull, down the dock, and over to where his working shrimp trawler was anchored. On the deck of the smelly ship were two men, equally as tall. Blizzard's brothers. Their ebony skin gleamed in the late afternoon sun.

"These pirates here are goin' to do the cleanin' for us today, bros'," said Blizzard. "They snuck in here while we was out shrimpin' and they've been pokin' where they shouldn't be pokin', so theys agreed to do our dirty work."

"But ... we ... need to get ... *home*," whined Guy in protest.

Blizzard turned and glared at Guy. He grabbed the collar of his shirt behind his neck and began walking forcefully with him off the boat, leaving Maddie.

He leaned over and whispered in Guy's ear: "Your daddy the magistrate, right boy?"

"Yes sir."

"I'll take you directly on home all right. I'm guessin' your daddy ain't goin' to be too happy 'bout his boy trespassin' ... doin' somethin' illegal ... on a black man's property at that. Doesn't look too good, know what I mean?"

Maddie ran in front of them and stood.

"Mr. Sims, sir. Please forgive us. We *will* clean your boat until it shines. Come on, Guy." She grabbed his hand and pulled him free from the strong hold of Blizzard's massive hand.

They spent the next hour up to their elbows removing the repulsive smell of warming shrimp dregs off the deck of the trawler.

It was the last time Guy had any inclination to play pirates on the rotting shrimp boats at Wallace Creek. It was not the last time acting landed him in a shadowed valley.

FIVE

Guy's ache to act became his dependency and eventually his curse. Yet, he lauded his parents for pushing him to pursue a path with promises of riches and admiration even though it drove him from his beloved marshes and Maddie. If they had not thrust him from Wynee with their praises and "bravos" for every private performance, off-the-cuff monologue, and leading act in school productions, he might have stayed and become stuck in some middling profession that no one noticed.

But they did push, for they recognized his "God-given talents," and they wanted him to glorify God by using them. So they said good-bye to him on a mid-summer's day and made him promise with one hand on the Bible that he would not forget to pray daily to his Maker, and that he would pledge to communicate regularly with them and with others in Wynee, mostly Maddie.

"I swear … I mean, I promise," he told them, and he had meant it.

God may have prepared Guy to become an actor, but he did not prepare him for Hollywood.

His parents had sent him to the Gold Coast with an adequate amount of money in his pocket so that he would be fairly comfortable until he found an agent and landed his first acting bit. But he knew, from reading about how some actors got their start that he might have to wait tables or be a lifeguard or something ordinary for a while until the right thing came along. He did not intend to waste his time for long though.

Guy's every nerve ending tingled with the want and anticipation of success as an actor. He vaulted out of bed every morning ready to take it all in and on. Every sight, sound, and smell was decadently foreign and enticing. His bloated southern vanity regarding his acting abilities, never once questioned or demeaned in Wynee, made him guilelessly, recklessly confident.

He soon found a tiny furnished studio apartment in North Hollywood. "It's hot and smoggy here in N.H.," said the landlord in too-tight pants, a cigarette dangling at the corner of his mouth as he talked. "We're hemmed in by the hills here in the San Fernando Valley. But the fresh ones, like you, can afford it and don't mind the sweat and bad air. Besides, you're close to everything."

Guy purchased some maps and learned the lay of the land. He picked up some actors' guides – Hollywood for dummies – and discovered that he was strategically situated at the right corner of a large square-shaped tract of territory that included the three important areas where the vast majority of studios, talent agencies, and casting directors are located: Hollywood/West Hollywood, and the west side, which includes Beverly Hills, Century City, Westwood, West L.A., Brentwood, Santa Monica, Culver City, and then his immediate neighborhood of Burbank, Universal City, Studio City, North Hollywood, and Van Nuys.

Guy was not the least bit frightened of Hollywood. He had been loved and sheltered in Wynee, so he naively maneuvered through the city, enamored and exuberant, as if it already adored him. He had no point of reference for anything to the contrary.

Initially, Guy took the bus. He soon ascertained that most LAers, if not cruising in a convertible, walked, jogged, biked, or motorcycled. The latter form of transportation appealed greatly. Somehow he imagined that riding astride a shiny chrome motorcycle fit his new "Guy Jamison" persona. *My signature.* He was already playing a role.

He called his parents, collect, and asked them to wire him a down payment on a used motorcycle. "Everyone gets around this way," he belied. He knew that their enthusiasm regarding his actually being in Hollywood overshadowed any concern they may have for his safety, as well as their reluctance to supply him with money in excess of what they had already bestowed.

They sent the money, and he found a Harley-Davidson low rider in like-new condition in a trader magazine. It sported plenty of chrome, large shiny pipes, and just a touch of dark purple with pin striping.

When he first arrived in Hollywood, he wrote to his parents and Maddie a few lines every day. He kept two yellow note-pads beside one another at his dining table and filled in a few sentences on each pad Monday through Friday. On Friday afternoons, he would mail both letters and start again.

> *"It's incredible out here! You think we've got palm trees in South Carolina, but they ain't* (scratched through with 'are not' written above) *anything like the California palms. They're huge! Every house is a palace, and the beaches - wow!"*

"Got my Harley. Don't worry. I'm driving safe. It's so cool though. You would love it."

"Found a job lifeguarding on the beach. Just have to take a training course. When I told them I was a South Carolina boy who lived near the water, that's all they seemed to need to hear. Had to take my shirt off for them too. (Strange.) Guess they don't want anyone with flab abs sitting in the life guard seat and giving them a bad name. This will be GREAT! It's only from 2:00 every day. I can stay in great shape saving people and do auditions in the mornings.

I got my headshot. Yeah. Everyone who wants to become an actor has to get one. This guy next door to me, Louis, he's been an extra in some movies and gave me info on what to do. He said, "You have to have a headshot." He gave me the name of some photographers. I went to this guy who charged $200 for only TWO 8x10s. Got one of me in my "I'm thrilled to be here" look, and the other with a more serious, action-star (ha! ha!) expression. I have to put the pictures together with my resume. I don't have much on my resume, except for those plays I did in Wynee, and that one time I was 'Oliver' in that production in Charleston. Guess I'll have to impress them with my great acting abilities in person! Ha! Ha! Pray for me!

No one had to pray long for Guy's success. His energy and single-minded focus gave him boundless confidence. *Brash* confidence, which only Hollywood could appreciate.

One of Guy's neighbors, Terrence, strikingly half African-American, half Japanese, advised Guy to pursue some work as an extra on movie sets. Self-assuredly, he told him that three consecutive days as an extra, even if he just stood there and did not say anything, might gain him his SAG card. He also insisted Guy get an agent. "You can't make it in this God-forsaken town without those snakes … evil necessities they are," he expressed. "Directors and producers in movies or television won't give you a sideways glance with no agent." He wisely assured Guy that if he could just get a solid part in a play in L.A. that agents were always looking for new talent in local playhouses.

"And you definitely can't be taken seriously around here unless you have membership in the Screen Actors Guild," Terrence told him.

Despite his supposed first-hand knowledge of the inner-working of Hollywood's intricate clock, Terrence – Guy soon learned – had been in Hollywood almost a year, and he had yet to work three consecutive days on any set. And, no agent represented him. Guy had no interest in work as an extra, in theaters, soap operas, commercials, or training films. He wanted to be a phenomenon in movies – someone that everyone talked about, admired, and recognized for his profound talents. The cliché movie star – but even more remarkable. Not the match, nor the candle, but the flame.

Before Guy had a chance to set Hollywood ablaze, his life could easily have been extinguished. He regarded God's grace immediately following the event, and again considered it after the accident in Wynee, but at no time in between did he acknowledge providence's protection.

In jeans and a white t-shirt, astride his low rider, Guy looked almost like a dark-haired James Dean. He thought that about himself. Whenever he passed anything that shot back his reflection, he stole a quick admiring glance. He headed down the Hollywood Freeway, onto Sunset Boulevard, and up LaBrea, searching for a studio to attend a rare open casting call for an action/adventure movie starring Harrison Ford. Without a decent resume, no agent, or any real connections, he still assured himself of landing a decent part.

They may reconsider Harrison Ford. Guy laughed at the brazen thought; then, fleetingly contemplated the possibility.

From LaBrea, he quickly realized a wrong turn onto a road not evident on his map. It was a narrow road, lined with cars. A large Spanish-style structure with a bell tower dominated one side; on the other was a gymnasium with a Spanish-style facade.

As he considered turning his motorcycle around and trying a different route, he caught a reflection of himself in one of the windows of a parked car. He drove slowly, picking up his mirrored image in window after tinted window. He did not see the crosswalk, or the children, or the rotund woman holding a stop sign until he was only a few feet from the scene. The crosswalk guard held the stop sign in front of her as if to shield herself from the impact; children scattered in different directions, bumping into one another in the chaos.

Horrified, Guy braked hard and turned his low rider into the side of a shiny silver convertible Mercedes. The impact thrust him, airborne, from his bike and landed him hard on his tailbone in the middle of the road.

The driver of the parked Mercedes sprung from her defaced car. Angrily, she inspected the large dent. She turned an icy glare toward Guy, who grimaced from the pain to his backside.

A female police officer hurriedly approached from the entrance of the building. The robust woman stood over Guy, cursing him. Children gathered around her, like chicks, wide-eyed, gaping down at him. He had his audience.

"Opps. I am sure enough in a pickle here," said Guy, grinning at awed children. "Sure enough." He stood gingerly, rubbing at his jeans. With Southern charm in full play, he asked: "Did you children see what just happened here?" He deliberately avoided eye contact with incensed adults.

"Lookee here children." He limped dramatically a few steps to his bike and turned it upright. "You see, I'm an actor. And I'm on my way to an important audition for an action movie, and this was just my chance to try an action move. I was never going to run over you. I just had this movie scene all worked out in my head, and I just got a mite bit carried away. Just a mite bit."

He acknowledged the mesmerized adults on the scene. He glanced from the officer to the Mercedes owner. "I am truly and lastingly sorry for all this commotion. I'm so glad no one was hurt. Of course, I will take care of any damages." Shrugging his shoulders and tucking his chin, he forced a sheepish smile.

Anger and annoyance dissipated from the Mercedes owner's face. She shook her head in disbelief. "When you're finished with the officer, son, I would like a word with you," she said firmly, but with a slight grin forming.

"Yes, ma'am!"

Although the officer had been ready, initially, to handcuff Guy and drag him into her parked police car, Guy's performance softened her. Some of the children still gathered around the motorcycle when she flipped open her ticket book.

"You're a *real* actor?" asked one of the children.

"What movies have you been in?" asked another, tugging at Guy's pants' pocket.

"Hey, I can see your underwear," said a freckled boy, pointing to a slight tear in his jeans – a result of the impact with the pavement. The children giggled and pointed.

"Okay, children, that's quite enough excitement for one day!" said the crosswalk guard. "I already heard the bell ring, so you're tardy for classes. Come along." She used her stop sign to herd the children back towards the school.

"Bye, kids! So sorry for the interruption!" expressed Guy.

"Do you know what could have happened here?" asked the officer, after the children were out of earshot. "Do you fully comprehend this situation?"

"Yes, ma'am. I do," said Guy, solemnly. "That's why I swerved my motorcycle into the car, to avoid the children." He glimpsed the Mercedes owner, her auburn hair pulled tightly into a pony tail, writing something in a notebook and staring at the dent in her car.

Guy focused back on the officer. "Do you have to arrest me?" he asked, dejectedly.

"I should, but I'm going to give you a ticket for not slowing down in a school zone and for the damage to the car. Let this be a warning to you."

"Oh, God has a way of gettin' … getting … my attention," said Guy, "and I definitely think this is one of those times."

"What's your name?" asked the officer.

"Well, it's interesting that you should ask, 'cause I'm in the process of changin' … changing … my last name. My legal name is Guy Olivier Rhett Butts, but I'm changing that last name to Jamison. Guy Jamison will be my name out here in Hollywood."

The officer put her head down to stifle a snicker. "Good idea." She strained a serious expression. "Well, all I need is your legal name, Mr. *Butts*," she said, lowering her head again to compose herself.

She filled out the ticket, gave it to him, and warned: "This is a long way from South Carolina, Mr. *Butts*. You won't last long out here daydreaming while riding your bike. Best do that while sitting out on the beach."

"Yes ma'am! Excellent advice. Have a nice day!" Guy called to her as she walked, smiling, toward her police car.

He looked over at the Mercedes owner, dressed in a stylish white, low-cut pantsuit, leaning against her damaged car; she intently surveyed Guy as he swaggered toward her.

"Ma'am, you have no idea how sorry I am to have defiled such a beautiful automobile. What can I do to make it up to you?"

"Did you happen to be on your way to the audition at Studio 17?"

He looked at her curiously. "Yes … ma'am. How did you know that?"

"Well, so was I after I dropped my daughter off here at school."

It seemed odd to him, with her expensive clothing and luxury car, that she would want – or need – a part in a movie. "You're auditioning too?" he asked.

She laughed. "No. I am an agent. Marsha Chambers." She extended a hand. "Do you have an agent?"

"No."

"What is your name?"

"Guy ... Jamison."

"Well, Guy Jamison. That was one helluva peformance I just witnessed. One of the best, I have to admit. If you have that much natural talent under pressure, then I cannot wait to see what you will do in front of a camera. Follow me to the studio."

For Guy, obtaining an agent was that easy. When Guy told his parents the story, leaving out that his vanity caused the accident, they just knew that God directed every move. This was affirmation that their Guy was in the right place doing what He intended for their son.

The open casting call was to weed out a new face to play Harrison Ford's sidekick for an action film. The director wanted an unknown, but someone with unmistakable, spontaneous charm. In a movie that boasted sold-out theaters nationwide in the first week, Guy naturally and effortlessly played the likeable, but cocky partner to the star's Bostonian detective role. Guy even absorbed the nuances of the tough accent as if it were his own from birth. Missing from the part was any trace of Guy's sweet iced tea upbringing.

The new "It Guy" was featured in magazines and interviewed on morning shows. Thrilled, Marsha introduced Guy to other main actors and major directors. He was invited to elaborate parties and intimate gatherings and handed a multitude of scripts to "consider". Not once did he falter; he was in his fish bowl breathing the water he was meant to breath. Guy said the right things to the right people, and he instinctively honed in on the specifics of the trade. He felt he had Hollywood in his grasp.

But the land of make-believe consumes.

Guy eased into the Hollywood scene on a breeze. Obscured by the clouds of his success were those once most important to him.

SIX

FATIGUED BY FRAGILE MEMORIES, Maddie left Guy's bedside in the middle of the afternoon to walk outside and breathe some fresh air. She needed to clear her head. She was thankful that at least the throngs of reporters had dispersed. A few still squatted in the hallway and in parked cars just outside the hospital's doors. She looked around to see if anyone was approaching her. The longer Guy convalesced in the hospital, the flatter his story became. Stu told her worldwide media checked in daily, asking about Guy's status. She assumed they would swarm again if he fully regained consciousness and began recovery.

Watching Guy sleep had nagged her mind with thoughts of their childhood. She stood at the entrance to the hospital and inhaled a prolonged breath in through her nose, pulled her rib cage up, and exhaled fully. A piercing screech overhead caused her to look skyward. An enormous red-tailed hawk circled. Its scream consumed the air above the hospital. Maddie's eyes spotted the object of the bird's distress – a smaller hawk perched on the hospital's communication tower. *Its mate?* Maddie fixated on the scene. Small, gray clouds formed directly above the quarreling birds. The rest of the sky was clear.

Maddie lowered her eyes, focused on another contemplative breath. She began walking. She decided to walk to Lollie's and buy one of the café's popular chicken salad sandwiches. She had missed lunch. The half-mile walk would clear her conscience.

Graying men in tired jeans occupied rocking chairs on Lollie's porch at the corner of Oak and Palm streets. They just seemed to always be sitting there: misshapen, well-worn hats, scruffy beards, and a half-empty bottle of Mountain Dew beside them. Some held a metal can for their tobacco spittle. A tattered, dirty checkers board with miscellaneous black and white chips waited on a side table. Maddie approached Lollie's, studying the men carefully for the first time. Some of the same men sat there during her childhood. Frozen-in-time fixtures on that porch – talking, spitting, and drinking. *Did they have careers? Families?* Observing them gave her an odd sense of security.

Lollie squealed when Maddie entered the store. Her hair, always too red, too short, and too tightly permed, made Maddie think of a clown.

"Girl! Where have you been? You don't come to see Lollie enough since you been a doctor here in this sorry town. Come here and give Lollie a hug!"

Her soft frame enveloped Maddie. *Her grandchildren probably adore her*, thought Maddie.

"You let me look at you! Girl, you look too tired. Just like I thought," she said shaking her head disapprovingly. "You're going to be a workaholic like your daddy. Jesus rest his soul. Don't you go on workin' yourself to *death* now. Work ain't worth that."

"It's not the work. It's the patient that be tirin' her out presently," said a voice from the back of the store.

Maddie recognized it right away as Miss Sumney's. She emerged from behind the aisle of candy and chips. She had a bag of Funions and a Mountain Dew in one hand and a packet of Red Man in the other.

"Ain't that right?" she asked Maddie. "Lord, child, you do look worn."

"I'll be all right, Miss Sumney," responded Maddie, stiffly.

"Lord, child, you knows you can call me Squash now that you's grown. I ain't your sitter no more and you ain't a wild little girl no more," she smiled. "Lord, child, you came home dirtier than any other white child I ever seen. You know what? When all them other girls were flittin' around town shoppin' the stores with big bows in their hair, you were up in some tree or in the marsh." She put her arm around Maddie and squeezed her bony frame close. "And now look at you. Who woulda ever known? Got you a big medical degree from the USC, and come back here to save all us folks. I can walk around with my nose stuck up high 'cause I practically raised you myself. Somethin' of my smarts rubbed off, ain't that right?" She squeezed Maddie again and grinned wider. "Uh huh. That's got to be it!" Maddie managed a smile. It felt good to be distracted, momentarily.

Squash released her hold on Maddie and set her items down on the tiled countertop. She took out her wallet.

"When you're finished ringing her up, I'd like one of your chicken salad sandwiches and some iced tea," said Maddie. "Then I need to head back."

Squash took the Mountain Dew out of the small brown bag, unscrewed the top, leaned back against Lollie's counter and took three long gulps. She wiped her mouth with the back of her hand and looked at Maddie.

"You know what the Word say about frettin'," Squash said to her.

"What?" asked Maddie, not as a question, but as an expression of annoyance. She suddenly felt eight and ready to brace herself for a lecture.

"I should have seen this comin' years ago when I tried to run that boy off, knowing who he belonged to. I told God then that if He was tryin' to have a sense of humor that He was way off. I knew it would break your daddy to know you was friends with him, after what happened. I knew you kept on bein' friends with him, but I just pretended I didn't know. Didn't want to make a big fuss outta somethin' that your hard-workin' daddy'd have to deal with."

"That's enough!" said Maddie, shooting a glance at Lollie, whose back was facing them as she prepared the sandwich.

"Lord, child, everyone in this town knows what happened way back then. When I told you after your daddy died a few years ago because you wouldn't stop beggin' to know, you musta been the only one didn't know. Thought sure someone'd slip and tell while you were a kid, but they done good. That boy lyin' up there's the only one who don't know the truth. Now he put his parents in the grave, and your daddy's in the grave, so it don't much matter anymore, do it?"

"Stop!" said Maddie. "Lollie, how long does it take to make a chicken salad sandwich?"

Squash set her items down on the counter and walked toward Maddie, grabbing her by both shoulders. "I'm not tryin' to upset you, child," she said softly. "I love you like you was my own daughter. You know that. I just want you to put what's happenin' in perspective. That boy ..."

"You know he's like a brother to me!" interrupted Maddie, defensively. "We spent practically every minute growing up together."

"Oh, he's much more than that, child," said Squash. "But he left this town and your life and his parents' lives, pursued his own – and badly, I must say – then pops back in here and 'spects we all bow down. Then he flat out does the unthinkable and now you're up there frettin' over him day and night."

"He has no one else."

"By his own choice. Listen, Maddie. Listen to what He's tellin' you in all this. Pay attention, but don't go frettin' and let your heart hurt over this. It ain't worth it. God's got it all worked out somehow. If the boy dies, there's some lesson in that. If he lives, there's some lesson there, too. Let Him take care of it, and you don't just go wearin' yourself out tryin' to make it all right."

"Amen," said Lollie, who plunked down the sandwich and tea on the counter.

A tear glided down Maddie's face. Lollie grabbed a tissue from behind the counter and approached her.

"You *needed* to come in here and get whooped up on by this pearl of wisdom," said Lollie, giving Maddie another embrace. "We love you. We just don't want you to lose yourself."

"I won't," said Maddie, resigned. "I promise." She reached into her pocket to pull out a $10 bill.

"Oh, no. That meal's on the house. And you just walk on down here next time you need a good fussin' at," said Lollie smiling. "If Squash ain't here, I'll try to come up with somethin' myself."

"I'm sure you will," said Maddie, managing to smile back. "You two take it easy on the next customer who walks through these doors."

"Lord, child, I'm spent after that," said Squash. "I need to go home and take me a rest."

Maddie walked out the door, said, "Have a nice day," to the men on the porch, turned her face toward the warmth of the afternoon sun, and began walking back toward the hospital. On her walk to Lollie's she had not noticed the air's thick perfume. With her senses cleared, she realized that the wisteria hung heavy from the telephone poles and trees. From the dense tangle of vines – eyesores during the winter months – cascaded copious blooms. Adding to the bouquet were bushes of daphne odora buzzing with energetic bees. Hyacinth bloomed blue, purple, and pink in the beds in front of homes.

Maddie thought of the elderly women at First Baptist crowded together at the entryway; Channel No. 9 clung to walls and enveloped the sanctuary. Just as some of their scent lingered on her for hours after she returned home from church, she wanted the fragrance of the spring flowers to drift with her into the hospital; it was a happy, hopeful smell.

She decided she would enjoy the early spring a while longer before joining Guy again. On a bench outside the hospital, she sat, placed her tea beside her, and unwrapped the sandwich. She thought for a moment about the encounter with Squash at Lollie's. Stubbornly, she desired to shrug off Squash's impertinence. But the words rang true. She spent waking thoughts on Guy, their past together, his present condition, and the uncertainty of his future. In sleep, she stumbled exhaustedly through doors that led nowhere.

After Guy left for Hollywood, Maddie drenched herself in him. When she read his letters, she imagined where he might be at that given moment. She prayed for his day when she woke up each morning. She passed on snippets of humorous or interesting news she learned from Squash or her daddy about Wynee.

> *Lula left her door open to the card shop one day to let some fresh air in and a baby alligator came in and just about took Tubby. You know, that fat cat that she lets live at the shop?*

I see Mater all the time here at USC, but when I call
out "Hi, Mater," he gives me the evil eye and takes me aside
and tells me he's changed his name to Matt while he's here
at school. I just keep on acting like I'm forgetting though.
Makes him so mad. I think he really thinks it's funny,
though. He's still sweet on that girl Cilly that he met last
summer in Wynee. You know, the one who moved to Wynee
after we graduated. They'll probably get married one day.

When I talked to Daddy on the phone the other night,
he said Spokes was telling the biggest whopper of his
shrimping career. Said this time that a giant white shark was
stuck in the river and that it came after his boat and bit a
huge hole in the net to get at a catch of shrimp. Sure enough,
Daddy said there was a hole. But no one believes a white
shark could survive in that river.

Maddie wrote to Guy and occasionally talked to him on
the phone. She ached for their lives to remain connected,
nagged all the while with the reality that they would not. His
letters to her slowed, and then stopped, when he began acting
in his first movie. He occasionally jotted her a short note to
say, "Sorry. So busy. Having tons of fun!"

The Buttses telephoned Maddie at her dorm to tell her that
Guy had written a long letter with the details of his first movie
acting experience, and to announce the movie's release date.
They were thinking of flying out to California to surprise Guy
at the premier of his first movie. Would she like to come? She
would, she told them, if she could work it out with her professors.

As the movie premier date approached, Maddie flitted
around the campus, charged – and anxious – at the thought
of seeing Guy.

A few days before their departure, the urge to call Guy
was so pronounced that she felt physically prodded. After an

afternoon class ended, she went back to her dorm and dialed his number. He was home. It was mid-day in California.

"Hey, Guy!"

"Maddie! How are you?"

"I'm great. I wanted to know how the ..."

"Hey, Maddie, remember the actress from that show 'Too Many Kids' we sometimes watched together? The cute little blond girl that was always saying those funny lines?"

"Well, yes ..."

"She's here, right now! In my apartment! Of course, she's grown up now. She's actually our age. Her name's Christy Sheely. That's actually her name. She didn't change it when she became an actress. She's here because she was in that movie I just made. We've just been talking about what a great experience it was. Cool, huh!"

"Yeah, cool. Hey, Guy ..."

"You just wouldn't believe how many interesting and famous people I'm meeting every day now. That movie is really launching my career! And I've got a whole stack of scripts that I'm supposed to read and decide ... I actually get to decide ... what I'm interested in, my agent said. Can you believe that?"

"That's just so great for you. I'm so thrilled ..."

"And I'm moving because I got a ton of money from doing that movie. Not as much as Harrison Ford, of course. Not even in the ballpark, but a lot for me. So I'm going to move into a little nicer place in a nicer area. I'll make sure I give you my new address and phone number."

"Guy, how would you feel if your parents and I came out there some time to visit you?" she blurted out quickly, before she was interrupted again by Guy's enthusiasm.

"Oh ... well, that would be great. But ... uh ... now is not the best time. When were you thinking? I'm just swamped right now and my agent said we need to decide on the next movie right away, so that means I'll be on the set somewhere around here or on location. What I really want to do is be on location somewhere fun!"

"No particular time frame," said Maddie.

"I'll let you know when a good time is, how about that?"

"Sounds good. Hey, I'll let you go back to your guest."

"Okay. Hey, Maddie?"

"Yeah?"

"You didn't tell me how classes are going. Have you gotten to dissect anything fun lately?"

"No, just still taking all the ..."

"Oh, Maddie, there is someone knocking on my door. I'm sorry. Can I talk to you a little later?"

"Sure."

"I'm glad you called. Bye, Zipp!"

Maddie called the Buttses shortly after her conversation with Guy and persuaded them to reconsider their surprise trip to California. She framed it in such a way that Guy's parents understood perfectly the hectic demands of a talented actor rocketing toward stardom. Of course it wasn't a good time, they said. They would wait for his invitation.

It never came. For the first two years, Maddie and Guy's parents received sporadic postcards from some of his movie locations with a scribbled note about when his next movie would be released. *Be sure to watch*, he always instructed. He rarely called his parents and never called Maddie. They dialed Maddie immediately after Guy telephoned them to tell her what he said, and always added, "He said to tell you 'hello' and that he misses you." At first she believed them.

Lawrence Butts decided that the best way to keep up with news about his son was to subscribe to some of the Hollywood rags. Any mention of Guy was clipped and stuck in a folder, which was then thrust at Maddie each time she returned home for a visit.

For a while she poured over the clippings, happy for any glimpse of Guy's life. Reviews were often positive: "The new 'Guy' hits every power-packed emotion dead-solid perfect. What a natural talent! What a find!"

Ultimately, the reviews and articles turned her stomach: "What a cutie, this Guy! He oozes with charm, has that little lilt of a Southern accent, and oh so handsome. Hollywood luvs Guy!"

The Buttses did not clip the articles featuring photography of Guy with his shirt off, Guy with a blonde on his lap, or Guy cavorting on the beach with a buxom brunette. But Maddie had seen some of them on magazine racks in the grocery store or in the USC bookstore.

She told no one at USC that she knew Guy. Most often, reports of him told of his "Southern upbringing," but rarely mentioned Wynee. So no one, except for Mater, knew there was a link. Mater seemed to know intuitively not to inquire on the subject when occasionally crossing her path on campus.

When Maddie's college friends brought up the subject of Guy over hot dogs at Sandy's or pizza at Mellow Mushroom, she attempted to redirect the conversation.

"He's just amazing to watch," cooed Carla. "I went to see his new movie three times just to soak it all in."

Maddie rolled her eyes. "Isn't there a folk band playing later at ..."

"Oh, he's dreamy! I'd just love to run my hands through that hair of his," expressed Trisha-Anne.

Maddie's face contorted in disgust.

"You don't like Guy Jamison?" asked Rainey, who was from California.

"He's a movie star!" blurted Maddie. "He's all right. Can our conversation be any shallower? Are we still in high school, or are we actually college students?"

Maddie ignored irritated expressions.

Throughout college and medical school, Maddie maintained regular contact with the Buttses, who seemed incessantly hopeful and fervent about Guy. Their painful smiles and fawning enthusiasm belied broken hearts. They reasoned away his infrequent phone calls. In private, they fretted and prayed, and continued to love their son – increasingly a stranger to them.

Maddie reluctantly pressed Guy into obscure crevices of her heart and mind. Eventually, there were days when she thought of him little or not at all. She dated mostly pre-med students; she even thought herself intensely in love with a Ugandan medical student named Benard while on a medical mission trip during her final year. Time and distance depleted the affair before it took hold.

Maddie absorbed herself in studies and training, Guy became a pleasant memory of her childhood. An element of their time together would surface at a peculiar moment – such as when she was studying the epithelial tissues of a cadaver. A spontaneous smile materialized and she remembered the time the two of them tumbled over the rotting remains of an enormous alligator near Duck Weed Pond. Guy had fallen directly in front of its gaping mouth dried wide open from the sun. She muffled a snicker as she thought of the girlish "eeeeeee" sound he made as he jumped up, embarrassed, and then walked off angrily in the direction of home without a word.

She thought of the same high-pitched squeal emoting from him when they were swimming in the river along the marsh and a straying enfant hammerhead bumped up against him.

She delighted in the thought of him scrambling frantically from the water.

She allowed herself to think of the Guy of their youth, not as he had allowed Hollywood to transform him.

However, Guy's father and mother, as his loving parents, would not let it rest. Exasperated with their prodigal son, they decided one day that "enough was enough." It was in her childhood home on Azalea Lane, which she inherited after her father died suddenly from a heart attack after one too many 30-hour shifts, that Lawrence met her one fall evening. He bounded into her yard, exuberant; she had just arrived home, exhausted and hungry, just like her father had for many years before. She wished Squash was waiting inside with a dinner of pecan chicken and rice.

"Maddie!" said Lawrence, approaching her with out-stretched arms. He acted as if he had not seen her in a while, though she saw them most Sundays in church and sporadically still dined at the Buttses home for Sunday lunch. "Maddie, I have some great news! I came up with a way to get Guy back here for a visit!"

"Oh?" Maddie braced herself.

"I went to Town Council and suggested that Wynee host a parade and celebration in his honor. They bought it: hook, line, and sinker. They admitted that it was a first for Wynee ... to have someone famous born here. Talked about having a plaque made for him down on Front Street to commemorate the event and to have a ceremony for the plaque dedication while he's here. The ideas were rolling!"

"Oh."

"Maddie. I thought you would be excited about this," said Lawrence, his expression darkening.

"Oh, I'm just ... tired," she lied. "It's a great idea. I just think you should be aware that ..."

Lawrence lightened again, interrupting Maddie, "They're going to send out an official letter with the Wynee Town Council letterhead to invite him! It's being planned for the spring! Not too far away. Charlene's going to be so happy about this!"

"I'm sure she will be," managed Maddie.

Physical, prolonged distance from her only son had altered Charlene. Although high-spirited and unscathed exteriorly, Charlene's odd escapades became more bizarre the longer he stayed away. All the trees around the couple's home hung heavy with bottles, and chair hell was filled to the brim after years of roadside collecting. The next avenue of escape, when she was not in church, at the movies, or catering, was to garden – frenzied and thoughtlessly. She purchased every conceivable and available flowering plant and stuck them wherever she could dig a hole in her massive yard. Once established, the landscape became a flowering jungle, sheltered from the town by wild beauty and fragrance. She explained away her latest obsession by saying she needed the flowers to decorate her cakes and tables during catered events. Wyneeans attributed her offbeat style of gardening to her Northern roots. Her Yankee blood was to blame for peculiarities.

"I think it's a great idea, like I said before," managed Maddie. "I just want you both to realistically be aware that his schedule may not allow for it at the time that you're thinking about. Just prepare yourself ..."

"The Town Council is setting it up for a weekend in April, when everything is beautiful and in bloom ... so the media can see how lovely Wynee is ... where Guy originated, and that's that," said Lawrence, his demeanor hardening. "He'll come, or the media will report that he did not even show up for his own hometown honorary day. He'll be here!"

"Oh," said Maddie simply, stifled by his desperation; she hugged Lawrence and added, "Keep me posted." She called after him: "Thanks for letting me know."

Maddie entertained no hope that Guy would accept Wynee's invitation. She prayed that his parents' hearts would not be shredded. She felt both irritation and compassion for their ache. While she attempted to seal off Guy from her heart and mind, their efforts pried. When she found her conscience wandering into a scenario that involved Guy, she chastised herself, forcing intention and focus in her work at the hospital.

She neglected to share the news with Stu, in whom she had gradually become interested since he arrived in Wynee months earlier to "rescue" the fledgling hospital. Stu had attended the Riley Halls boarding school on the outskirts of Wynee for one year when he was only eight to settle a dispute his Atlanta parents instigated with their friends regarding whether or not a child of such a young age actually had the stamina and intellect to 1) be away from his home for that long and, 2) sustain high grades in an academically challenging environment. Stu did not disappoint; his success in the lowcountry school became a repetitive topic of conversation among Atlanta's tight socialites.

Despite his elitist, pompous upbringing, Stu fondly remembered the year in South Carolina. He told Maddie, after they became friends, that it was the motherly affection of a Mrs. Walker, the guidance counselor, who affected him most. Maddie had gasped, and Stu's response was a hand affectionately placed on her shoulder. He asked her if she was okay.

"She was my mother," said Maddie, quietly.

"Oh. I had no idea ... She went out of her way to speak kindly, or to give me a hug. I didn't get either from my own mother. She always asked me what my 'high note' was for the day. I inquired about her when I first moved here and someone told me she had died in an accident not long after I left the school."

"Yes," said Maddie, divulging only: "I was a baby."

A Duke graduate, Stu could have practiced anywhere other than Wynee. She knew his salary must only be a fraction of his worth. Before she learned of his connection to her mother, she surmised that he must consider Wynee a missionary-type experience. His stint in Wynee was most likely temporary. But the fact that her mother inadvertently helped draw him there spurred an attraction.

Maddie let Stu in by degrees. Almost nine years her senior, his stalwart, patient nature reminded her of her father. She slowly revealed to him elements of her childhood with Guy and her relationship with the Buttses. She did not tell him how and why her mother had died. But their relationship progressed and she felt that, quite possibly, there might be a future with Dr. Stu Ledger.

Maddie kept quiet about Wynee's plans to roll out the red carpet for Guy. Stu learned soon enough and asked her if she knew.

"Yes."

"Why hadn't you mentioned it?" he asked.

"Because I don't think it's important. I doubt, seriously, that Guy will come back to Wynee. He hasn't been here in years. Hasn't even invited his parents out to see him … parents who haven't done anything to deserve that kind of treatment."

Sensing her tension, he asked, "Would you be okay about it if he did come for a visit?"

"Of course," she said, busying herself with charts, avoiding eye contact.

He studied her.

She added uneasily: "For the Buttses' sake, I hope he does come back. They *need* to see him."

Still watching her, Stu said nothing.

Maddie stopped writing and looked at him. In a low, firm whisper so that the nurses would not hear, she said, "We were friends ... almost like siblings. I've told you that. It's not threatening, if you're worried about *us*, for him to come here! But he won't."

The discussion dropped.

A few Sunday mornings later, First Baptist's lawn buzzed with the feverish news that Wynee's own movie star would, indeed, return to grace his hometown with his presence. A swarm of squealing teenage girls accosted the Buttses before they reached the church's threshold.

Buoyantly, Lawrence broke away from the wriggling pack and met Maddie as she approached the church. "We got a call from him late last night! You know it was only 10 in California. He said he was 'honored' ... '*honored*' to be invited back here for all kinds of celebrations! He said he would work it into his *busy* schedule."

Maddie glanced around and noticed others evaluating her reaction. Charlene walked up beside her husband.

"Oh, Maddie ... isn't it wonderful news? And, you know, he told me over and over again how sorry he was that it had been so long," Tears formed on the lower rims of her eyes.

Lawrence, beaming, wrapped an arm around his wife.

"I'm so happy for you both that it's working out," managed Maddie.

"For us?" said Lawrence. "What about for you? Won't you be happy to see him, Maddie?"

"It will be nice to see him," she said, smiling dryly.

Before they had a chance to question her demeanor, she was saved by the church bell. They were to enter the church in quiet reverence. Temporarily, Maddie eluded further talk about Guy Olivier Rhett Butts Jamison.

SEVEN

I T   W A S   M A D D I E ' S   V O I C E Guy heard; her face in the fog.
"Just rest," she had said, and her face disappeared again. He
was in a real hospital. He *was not* on a film set. He slowly eased
his head to one side, forced a sliver of light through weighted
eyelids, and registered a blurred IV. Pain stirred his nervous
system; he recognized his own moans rising from his chest.
A blanketed sensation calmed him back into dreams and
remembrances.

He dressed for his trip home. He pulled old clothes from
the bottom of a contemporary egg shaped cabinet. They were
clothes he had arrived in years earlier: loose-fitting Levis, an
old faded USC t-shirt, and a Panthers cap. It was to be his
"disguise" while traveling to the southeast.

Guy remembered dragging from under his white wave-
shaped bed the leather bag his father gave him as a high
school graduation present. He pulled a few shirts and pants
from high shelves in his walk-in closet. Stuffed in some underwear and socks. Exhausted, he moved about sluggishly. The
night before had been a late night. *They were all late nights in*

California. He looked forward to the red-eye flight; a few drinks and an eye mask would provide needed rest.

I'm resting now, he thought. A morphine-induced shroud anchored him to the hospital bed. Snippets of an off-color life floated in and out on a tide …

At his 5,000-square-foot Mediterranean-style home on a cliff in trendy Santa Monica, with its four bedrooms and large commercial-grade kitchen that he never used, Guy's bedroom floor was strewn with a few empty rum bottles, sundry clothing items – mostly his, but a pair of size 00 jeans and a lacy camisole belonging to his latest model turned actress – as well as a few pages of a script and some CDs. He glanced around. *What would my mother think?* – a vague thought, but then he let go a burst of hoarse laughter.

"Ha! Maria will get all this! Nothing to worry about, Momma. Got it all under control," he mumbled exhaustedly to no one.

He recalled picking up his boarding pass off the black granite countertop in the kitchen and grabbing the phone to leave a message for his publicist. But Fran was already in the office.

"That's right, Fran, it's just a few days of R&R, and I *don't* want to make it public."

"I know that after what's happened, it could be good for my image, Fran," Guy told her. "It's always about *that*, isn't it? When my image is bad, it needs to be good. When my image is too goody goody, it needs to have an element of bad.

"They'll learn about it soon enough and be stampeding down there. I just don't want to give it to them up front. Let me *breathe* for a few days!"

The latter sentence he said loudly and harshly. He quickly apologized and ended the conversation.

As he waited to board his plane and tried to remain inconspicuous, he thought he heard the clicking of a camera shutter. He carefully looked up from a newspaper he was pretending to read and saw no one with a camera aimed at him. It must be his paranoia and fatigue, he decided. He wanted to be left alone, just this once, and he felt that he might resort to Sean Penn-like fierceness if any paparazzi were to swarm in on him at that moment.

Since the success of his first movie, so soon after his arrival in Hollywood, he had been at the mercy of crafty photographers and sensational journalists ravenous for any morsel of his life. In a sort of sink or swim initiation, he learned their unscrupulous methods – the Herculean lengths to call attention to any tidbit in his life.

Advice from all those "in the business" closest to him was the same: "Either play it up for publicity, or don't put yourself into a situation that you don't want everyone to know about."

The attention was great when there was a new movie to promote. But the never-ending sound of camera shutters clicking and the in-your-face attitude of the paparazzi was unnerving to Guy. They were there when he exited a public restroom, walked into his dentist's office, or – heaven forbid – tried to eat a meal in a public restaurant. No matter how secretive or incognito while dating someone, they were always there.

The fans were different, although some could be obnoxious. They were mostly kind and appreciative if he granted them an autograph or spoke to them. Sometimes throngs of girls would squeal and point and then crowd around him before he could escape. He generally felt admired and supported by his fans.

He believed the paparazzi were out to destroy any semblance of character he possessed. He prickled brusquely at the thought. More often than not, he concealed himself when he left his home. Sometimes it worked; sometimes not.

"It's the price you pay for fame," was the common retort, if ever he complained.

A high price, thought Guy many times.

The flight attendant lingered near him a little too long when serving him coffee. He pulled his cap down farther over his forehead and excavated his Wynee drawl in an attempt to eliminate from her mind any shred of thought that she might be in the presence of a movie star.

"Thank ya kindly ma'am," he said to her in a goofy un-Guy Jamison way, to further waylay any suspicions.

She served him a beer and moved on. He stared out the window and listened to the Top 100 while dozing on and off. He thought about the desperate tone in his father's voice when calling about Guy Jamison Day.

"A parade ... oh, and banners ... and, yes, I'm sure there will be all kinds of parties in your honor. Your mother, Guy, she's fit to be tied ....We know you're always so busy ... we understand, son ... but your mother certainly needs to see you here on your special day. It's been far too long, you know … not that we don't understand the demands on you."

A twinge of guilt. Yes, it had been too long, but did they really understand the sacrifices he made? Guy Jamison Day. An honor. He couldn't dispute that, even if it was in his native postage-stamp town. As he stared at clouds meandering past the head-sized window, he clearly felt more than a pang of remorse for not visiting his hometown since experiencing stardom. He owed it to Wyneeans. They were fans too. He owed it to his parents, especially. He needed to see his parents.

Guy had told his father he would check his schedule. He did and realized he would have just wrapped up filming for a black comedy, his first. In the weeks after the Wynee visit he was to film in Vancouver for a small-budget artsy piece to be submitted to the Sundance Film Festival. All the top stars were "giving back," offering their time to acting in movies created by rising film students.

"Yes," he told his father. "I'll plan to be there."

His father had asked briefly about Skylark, his former fiancée. "No. Over, dad."

He grinned at the thought of taking *her* to Wynee. That certainly would have caused a stir. No traveling covertly with her at his side.

When they were together, Guy had not divulged much information about his past, except that he had a "great" upbringing and his parents were "wonderful and understanding" and that he grew up in the South.

"Southern California?" she had asked, in her thick Italian accent.

Obviously, she was unfamiliar with U.S. geography, so Guy kept it vague. "The other side of the country," he told her.

Guy came to know Skylark at a swanky Hollywood party. She was the new "it" girl. A model, with shiny, raven hair. She had left a scandalous affair with a famous, but much older and very married, Italian filmmaker to escape to the states and birth her illegitimate son. Her beauty and curvaceous form overshadowed any moral indiscretions.

A few weeks with a personal trainer after the birthing experience and Skylark was in the Hollywood game fielding a barrage of calls regarding roles for seductive women. Wholesome, God-fearing citizens may have offered her a down-cast eye for coveting another woman's husband and for bearing that man's child out of wedlock, but Tinseltown revered her and collaborated to make her their next glitzy star.

Shortly after a brief meeting, Guy learned she was cast to star as his femme fatale in an updated version of a 1960s spy thriller. Before the film was well into production, the two were an item. He had dated American actresses since ensconcing himself in Hollywood, but this international beauty enthralled him.

Guy Jamison lost all sense of decorum. He was photographed licking frosting off her shoulder after she popped out of a cake, scantily clad, for his 27th birthday. He was photographed holding her baby on a beach in France while she sunbathed nude beside him. A "close" friend of the couple's reported to *Scoop* magazine that they were "very happily" sharing his abode.

Sky is the Limit for Guy
Guy's Head is in the Clouds for Sky
Lark Shares Nest with Guy

The headlines were endless.

Soon enough, there were close-ups of a diamond ring on Skylark's left ring finger.

Guy had downplayed the sensationalism of the relationship when he told his parents of the engagement.

"She's really just a nice girl who got herself into a bad situation," he told them, making it sound like he was rescuing her in good ol' boy Southern fashion. "Don't believe everything you see or read. They're just trying to sell magazines. She's sweet and you'll just love her little boy."

The Buttses never had an opportunity to meet their future step-grandchild. Guy's relationship with his intoxicating co-star fizzled with the same fury as it had begun. The media, in fact, was voracious in pursuit of the failed lovers.

The more disgusted Guy became regarding the coverage of Skylark's reconciliation with her son's father – who left his wife and headed to the West Coast when he learned of the seriousness of her engagement – the craftier the photographers and reporters. One such deplorable team posed as a husband and wife pushing a baby carriage. It turned out that under the baby blanket was hidden the camera equipment and the reporter's notebook. When Guy was seen grabbing Skylark's arm at a park in a last ditch effort to persuade her, the strolling couple grabbed their paraphernalia and encroached.

Guy angrily raised his hand to stop the photographer while simultaneously shouting insults at him and yelling for Skylark to not walk away. The report and the photos represented an incensed actor, pitifully ill-equipped to handle rejection.

On the rare occasions that Guy called his parents, they gently preached to him about his apparent falling away from Christ-like behavior … the abandonment of his decorous upbringing. They warned him about his decadence, and asked him to focus on his craft and not succumb to the ills of the culture. Their words fell on ears made deaf by the heady melody of success. His behavior, though shocking to everyday citizens, was customary – even expected – by his Hollywood peers.

"Isn't this what you wanted?" were piercing words to his parents when he bitterly called to tell them his engagement was off. When they chastised him for the perceived assault on the reporter, he circumvented with, "They are just looking for ways to sell magazines! It's all fabricated."

Though he recognized the subtle and gradual wounding of his adoring parents' hearts, he rationalized that they were proud of him anyway. "*God* gave all this to me," he blasphemed during that same conversation. "Of course you wouldn't want me to let *Him* down and not live my life as all successful movie stars do." He was certain of his mother's gasp when he exhaled those words. *Screw it*, he thought. Hollywood was great at sweeping wet blankets under its glitzy pall.

Not long after the Skylark episode, another cliché beauty cozied up for photos on Guy's lap.

Guy settled himself down into his first-class seat and considered his father's appeal to return home. It was the right time. Get away from the ugliness of his fiasco engagement. Experience a dose of Southern-style reality. Make up for lost time with his parents. Show them that he was still the good guy – the son that makes them proud.

He arrived in Charleston somewhat rested and relatively unscathed. The flight attendant had finally whispered to him that she *knew* who he was and was not going to divulge his identity, but would he *mind* signing a napkin for her. He obliged, smiled, and thanked her for her discretion.

He kept his head low as he exited the airport, pulling out dark sunglasses from his bag. Hurriedly, he picked up the black convertible Mustang rental car waiting for him and drove down Savannah Highway and onto U.S. Hwy. 17 to get out of busy Charleston and onto the quiet lowcountry back roads toward Wynee.

Compared to Los Angeles, the cars seemed to be crawling. Surroundings looked small, vacant. He eased back onto a pleasantly warm day. Clear. No wind. The air fragrant. In front of every home were hedges of azaleas radiant with fuchsia, purple, and pink blooms.

Guy passed a small field of unpicked cotton, forgotten during the fall harvest. The withered, dusky, drying stalks merged with the dark soil so that the ghostly tufts of white seemed suspended like a thick snowy cloud hovering just inches above the ground.

"I wish I were in the land of cotton. Old times there are not forgotten ..."

He smiled. The South was creeping in unsolicited. The tune in his head suddenly made him think of Maddie. He had thought briefly about her when he agreed to come back to Wynee. But he doubted she would be happy to see him, and he really did not want the burden of any unpleasantness. He was returning to Wynee to be esteemed, not confronted. *Yes*, he should have called her himself instead of just letting her receive the information from his parents. He should have informed her he was coming in early and that he desired to see her. *Hell*, he should have kept in better touch with her all these years. He considered momentarily how appalling his treatment of her had been.

Guy pulled his car to the shoulder of the road in front of a decaying cotton field. No homes nearby; no cars passing. Miles of fields, with a tree line as a distant backdrop. He got out of the car and walked to the edge of the field. A tuft of cotton hung precariously by a shred of its fiber. He stooped down and easily picked it. *Why did it not blow away in one strong gust of wind?* He held the airy tuft in his hand and rolled it around, feeling the hard seeds within. He lingered dreamily, wondering if jet lag was the reason for this pensive pause.

Walking back toward his car Guy noticed an ill-constructed, fading billboard across the road from where he had parked. Positioned in front of a crooked barn topped with rusting tin, the sign's large hand painted letters bellowed the message: *Hell is no place to be! Give yourself to Jesus now!* Guy chuckled and looked around – half expecting the Savior himself to be standing in the middle of the cotton field pointing a finger at him.

EIGHT

WHEN GUY DROVE into his unobtrusive hometown, he was met with no human fanfare. Only the signs for the upcoming parade hung from the telephone poles. Banners that read "Welcome Home, Guy!" and "Celebrate Guy Jamison Day!" were stretched across the main roads. No one noticed him pull into his parents' driveway and park his rented Mustang in the old two-car clapboard garage hidden from view by impenetrable shrubs and unruly wisteria. He was a few days early. It was Wednesday. The parade was scheduled for Saturday morning. He had decided he would try to spend some quiet time with his parents before his fervor was unleashed. He owed them time. He had given them none in many years. Plus, as a movie star, he understood the nuances of creating an atmosphere of mystery. He felt sneaky and snub easing out of the Mustang.

It was mid-morning. The lawn still held its dew and a wisp of spring coolness blew in from the marsh. The marsh's sulfurous odor permeated Guy's sense. He stood at the entrance to the garage and inhaled deeply the opposing aromas of gardenias, lilies, and roses. Everywhere he looked was color. His mother had been busy while he was away.

Quietly, he walked into the mudroom, careful not to let the screen door slam, and then through the large white kitchen. He heard his mother's loud humming from the adjoining dining room. The hum turned into a full-out whistle. No one could whistle a tune like his mother. *Amazing Grace.* He peeked around the door frame; her back to him, she arranged a large ivory vase with creamy gardenias. Her thick blond hair was wound loosely into a French twist at the back of her head. He watched her for a few moments. Guy's face flushed suddenly in an unexpected swell of emotion. Until then, he did not realize how much he missed his mother. He had been too busy, too consumed.

She stooped over and, midway through shifting into a favorite tune from "The Sound of Music," *Raindrops on Roses*, she ceased the music and drew in a deep sniff of the luscious blooms.

"Momma," said Guy softly.

Charlene swung around so abruptly that her arm swept the vase off the sideboard and onto the heart pine floor; creamy gardenias drowning in broken shards. Paying no attention to the catastrophe, she leapt over the mess and bounded into her only son's arms.

"Oh, Guy! You startled me! Oh ... I had no idea you would be here already." Tears saturated her cheeks, and she buried the wetness into his shoulder. Almost his height and amply framed, Charlene held Guy in such a grasp that he could scarcely breathe.

"Mo ... mma," he said, pulling her back gently and breathing deeply. "Let me look at you before you suck the life out of me."

"I guess you got your drama genes from me," she said, trying to compose herself, but only stifling her sobs. "But don't you know, Guy, how terribly .... *terribly* I've missed you. Did it have to be so long?"

With that, Charlene covered her mouth and held her hand up to Guy to excuse herself to a nearby bathroom. He winced at his mother's attempts to mollify her emotions. A burst of sobbing. Silence. Sniffs. Another torrent. Prolonged silence.

Guy sat down in one of the dozens of chairs in the room. He knew it would be traumatic after such a long absence, but the guilt confronted him sharply, piercing his gut. He tried to think of what he would say to his mother to comfort her.

Honor thy mother and father ... entered his thoughts just as his mother exited the bathroom, red-faced but composed.

"Momma ... I'm *so* sorry," said Guy, putting his arm around her. "I've been a wretch to be away so long. It was selfish and stupid, and I'm just ... sorry. Please forgive me."

"It's okay, son," she said. "You needed to make your way. You're here now and that's all that matters."

"It'll be different now," stated Guy firmly, yet not certain of its meaning or intention.

"Enough of that," said Charlene, forcing a smile. She put her arm around his shoulder and squeezed. She kissed him on the cheek. "Would you like some sweet tea? Probably haven't had any for a while! Made some homemade lemonade, too."

"I'll start with the tea and have some lemonade next. You can't really get either in California," said Guy, relieved that his mother was in better spirits. "None that's decent anyway."

Just as Charlene was plunking ice cubes into a tall glass, her husband entered through the mudroom door.

"Where is he? Oh my ... the Lord *is* good. Look at you!" Lawrence opened his arms wide and embraced fully. He patted Guy on the back and grabbed his biceps. His eyes glassed over with the threat of tears. He smiled wide, approving of Guy's strong physique – but said, "You look right worn out, son."

Releasing his hold on Guy, he stepped back and announced, "It's good ... really good ... *wonderfully good* to see you again." With that he put his arm around his wife, who struggled to restrain another crying jag. He just shook his head, as in disbelief, and stared at his son.

"I said this to Momma and I'll say it to you, Daddy, I'm sorry I stayed away so long. You've always been good parents and I have no excuse, except for career busyness. I'm going to do better."

"Son, we're just happy you're here safe and sound," said Lawrence.

"That's what I told him," added Charlene.

Charlene prepared three glasses of sweet tea and proceeded to the parlor with the glasses balanced on a silver tray. Guy and Lawrence were both seated in Queen Anne style chairs with slender cabriole legs and reupholstered seats. The finish on Guy's chair was a dark mahogany, while Lawrence's was lighter ash.

"It would be nice this time of year to sit on the front porch, but I don't expect you want to be bothered just yet by the townspeople," assumed Charlene, setting the tray down on a slight inlaid tea table.

"No one would ever see you with that jungle growing over the front porch," whispered Lawrence to Guy.

"What's that?" asked Charlene, turning to serve the glasses of tea.

"Said it's a pity we can't sit out there and enjoy the wisteria blooms," said Lawrence to his wife, smiling. When she turned to grab another glass, he winked at Guy and smiled.

As they talked and caught up about their lives, Guy studied his parents. Time and distance had allowed him an opportunity to see them fully for perhaps the first time. He never thought much about his parents' appearance, but they were handsome, no doubt. He had gotten his squared chin and straight nose from his father. His mother's gift was a full mouth and long eyelashes.

Whenever his father would reach over and touch his mother's shoulder or place his hand over hers, Guy imagined she stiffened somewhat before accepting the gesture with a slight smile. For his part, Lawrence praised and complimented his wife with the fervor of someone motivated by a remorseful conscience.

Guy studied mannerisms, personalities, traits, and expressions in order to better portray the characters he was hired to play. That was his job. He had not been attentive to such details while under their roof, but he evaluated every action and innuendo as he sat with them among the clutter of chair heaven.

"You could open up a specialty shop in Wynee and just sell chairs," he threw out, testing the water.

Immediately his father rolled his eyes, but then turned to his wife grinning and said, "She knows how to spot them!"

"Oh, Guy, you have to see what I did with your room," said Charlene suddenly, springing upward from her seat.

Guy saw her wink coyly at his father.

"Need to get some rest while you're back there," Lawrence instructed his son. "We can talk some more later. You look like you haven't slept since you left us," he added, putting a strong emphasis on "left."

Guy did feel as if he had not truly rested in years. His bones seemed to weigh more as he arose from the chair. The inner workings of his muscular, tan facade felt haggard, tattered even. His body felt as if it had already lived a lifetime. Being back in his parents' home was a serene continent away from Hollywood. Yes, he would withdraw to his room and rest for a while.

His mother paused at his bedroom door, an impish expression glided over her features before she turned the knob. What was a relatively plain room in his youth, with light blue walls, a quilt for a bed covering, and an antique mahogany bed and dresser, had been transformed into a tabernacle honoring his acting career. Movie posters decorated every wall. Stacks of photo albums and scrapbooks with every conceivable clipping from magazines and newspapers were neatly arranged and labeled. An action figure of his likeness, when he played CIA agent Lex Harwood, stood poised for combat on his dresser.

Guy sat on the bed, stunned.

"I'll be da ..."

"Don't you bring any of that Hollywood talk into this house," warned his mother sternly.

"I'm just not quite sure what to think about all this," he said, unsettled.

"We've been mighty proud of you, Guy. You know we had to be. And putting this all together ... keeping up with your accomplishments in movies and what you were doing with your life out there ... well, it just made me feel closer to you," she said, her voice strained. "You like it, don't you, Guy?"

"Well ... yes. It's a little overwhelming, but ... yes."

"Oh, honey. I'm just so, so glad you're home," said Charlene, smothering Guy into another bear hug. Feeling the onslaught of more tears, she managed, "You rest. I'll prepare some food." With that, she closed the door behind her, leaving Guy surrounded by his image.

His head swirled as he looked around the room. He had flown thousands of miles from Hollywood to be closed into a concentrated version of his chaotic life. He kicked off his shoes and reclined on a pillow. Was that really him on those posters, in the magazines? *Surreal.* When he thought of the time leading up to his departure from Wynee, it seemed sluggish, like a warm afternoon lounging in an Adirondack chair. In contrast, his movie career was a blip, devoid of any real sensory input – fast-forward frames that brought him to his room, where a compilation of that blip was on display.

As he tried to relax, his thoughts drifted unexpectedly to Maddie. A brief instance of her entered his mind when the Jesus sign confronted him at the cotton field. Here she was again. His thoughts turned to a time in his room when he was 11. Maddie challenged him that she could make a God's eye faster and better than he could. They had just come back from Vacation Bible School and had learned to make the Popsicle stick craft woven with a myriad of woolen strings – all a different hue.

"I don't need to make another one," he told her. "I just made one at church. It's just about as perfect as they come. Looks better, in fact, than the one the teacher made."

"Ha! It's pitiful. It's all loose. And you used too much black. You want a *black* eye watching over you? I can make one ten times better than that pathetic sight," she taunted, knowing that he would take the bait.

She ran to the kitchen, rummaged around in a draw, and brought back Charlene's baking timer. She wound the timer, spastically scattered the different colored yarns and the Popsicle sticks on his bed and yelled "Go!"

Maddie insulted teasingly while his fingers fumbled to wind the yarn. Minutes later she bested him, then proceeded to rib him mercilessly.

Would she be happy to see him? Surely she understood why he had to be away so long. *Sure she'll be happy.* He was glad she had achieved her goal to become a doctor.

They had not communicated over the past few years; when they did talk early on, the comfort level waned. He knew about her life mostly through his parents. As he rested there, heavy and fatigued, compunction nudged. *Why should I feel guilty?* He was one of the most successful young actors in the country.

Guy closed his eyes and thought about Maddie a few moments longer – her infectious laugh, her bright eyes. Would she still have that girlish playfulness? Would their former closeness override his contemptible behavior? Guy slowly opened his eyes. They adjusted and fixed on a colorful God's eye hanging from a short piece of fishing line from his ceiling light. A gentle breeze from the open window blew the eye so that it twisted from side to side, watching him. He beheld the room again. Dozens of Guy's eyes stared back at him. He was watching himself. Disconcerted, he eased his way off the bed and quietly opened the door. Surreptitiously, he glided into the guest room next to his. He slipped under the matlaisse cover, careful not to disrupt the rarely inhabited vignette.

Guy awoke to boisterous laughter.

"Ha-ha! He's here, ain't he, Ms. Charlene? He's here. I know it. Can't hide him from ol' Mater. I seen that sporty car hidden in your garage. I won't tell nobody. I know he ain't supposed to be here yet."

Mater had come to inspect a paint job that his crew had completed on the exterior and interior of the Butts's garage. When he saw the car, he barged into the house uninvited. Charlene mildly protested, smiling at Mater's teasing. She had long been a fan of Mater Sumney and his pleasing ways.

"He is here, but he's resting," she tried to say. "Just let him rest ... just a little."

"Where is he now?" ignored Mater. "That boy ain't been home in so long, we got about a month's worth of crabbin' and catchin' up to do."

Guy jumped quickly out of the guestroom bed, smoothed the powder blue cover, and snuck back into his room just before Mater entered the hallway. Guy opened his bedroom door to greet Mater and closed it behind him. He didn't want him to see the shrine his mother had created.

"Mater!" said Guy, reaching out his hand for a shake. "Knew that voice couldn't belong to anyone else."

Mater slapped Guy's hand away and grabbed him around the neck into a headlock. "Well, I'll be ... you look just like that big-shot star I heard about from the movies. Ain't never wasted my time or money seein' any of the movies that actor's in, but I heard about him." He said this as he released his muscular dark arms around Guy's neck and jabbed him in the ribs with his elbow.

"Ha-ha," said Guy, gasping for air. "Great to see you too, Mater."

"Hey, now, I go by Matt since my Gamecock days. Didn't Maddie tell you that? Oh, she tried to convince everyone to call me Mater ... thought it was funny ... but I threatened with bodily harm if anyone called me that. Mater was fine when I was a kid, but you know that Matt is more manly ... more sophisticated." He flashed a smile at Guy.

"Besides, my wife, Cilly – remember her that last summer we was together before you moved? Well, she needs to be able to hold her head up in town when she's talkin' about her fine husband," he said. "And my children have got to be proud of their daddy!"

"My parents mentioned you got hitched and then knocked her up a few times," retorted Guy.

"Oh, yeah, I'm an honest man makin' an honest livin' with a real family," said Mater, poking Guy in the ribs. "Thought that anywhere but here's where I wanted to be when I was growing up, but learned while I was away at school that I have a few things to offer this town and it had some things to offer me. So I've got me a pretty, pretty wife, and a business of my own."

"And I have children with real names," he added, laughing. "Decided the fruits and vegetables legacy was ending with me!" He laughed harder.

"Come on now, you boys," said Charlene. "I've got the best chicken salad in Wynee in the kitchen waiting for you – and some strawberry shortcake with homemade whipped cream if you eat your lunch."

"Now, that's what I'm talkin' about," said Mater. "This is exactly why I had to come and inspect that paint job at lunch time, Ms. Charlene ... just to be honest with you."

"I'm onto you Matt!"

Guy realized he was ravenous.

"You look like a marsh breeze could blow you into Georgia," observed Mater. "People don't eat in California? And you got enough dark stuff under your eyes to make people think you're trying to turn black. People don't sleep there neither? We'll get you right fixed up in Wynee. Yes sir, Mr. big shot movie star."

NINE

CANISTERS OF MEMORIES reeled for almost two weeks until Guy progressively opened his eyes with the intention of keeping them open for a while. Maddie was not there. As if emerging from a murky cavern, his mind recalled various fragments of present reality. He remembered forcing his eyes open and seeing her image in a haze. He felt her touch on his hand and heard the soothing tone of her voice.

Suddenly a nurse entered. Annette had been a fixture at the Wynee hospital practically since its foundation. Oblivious to Guy's consciousness, she went about her business opening curtains, scribbling her name on the dry erase board, and checking the chart. When she finally looked at her patient, she started and gasped.

"Oh! My heavens. You're awake!"

He struggled to articulate the word, "Hello," in his dry-as-Saltines mouth. What emerged was "Duhdo".

"Honey, you need some water before you try and say 'howdy do' or 'good mornin' or any such thing to me," said Annette, cheerfully. "When you don't use it, you sorta lose it. Know what I mean?" She smiled at him while filling a plastic cup in the sink next to the bed. She found a flexible straw and held it to his mouth.

"Just try to take a sip of this and run your tongue around in your mouth and over your teeth," she told him. "Then take a few more sips. You had a lot of swelling on your face and around your mouth ... lost a few teeth even, so you've gotta get it workin' again."

Guy's stomach clenched as Annette held the cup and her eyes lingered on his face. Her smile was forced and her eyes became glassy. *Is it that bad?* He wanted to ask her for a mirror, but worried another verbal attempt would fail. *Where's Maddie? What has happened to me?*

"You know," said Annette, making conversation as she set down the cup of water and evaluated Guy's vitals. "People around here said you were ... uh ... are ... a pretty good actor. Say you've made some decent flicks. Well, I don't see movies myself so I can't give you a critique one way or another. I prefer karaoke. Do they have that in California? I have to say there is a fine karaoke establishment right here in Wynee. Haven't been able to get there in a while, though. Workin' too much and too hard. They probably didn't have it back when you lived here. Bill Wolfe owns it. Interesting man. Got a giant wolf tattoo on his chest, and ... I hear ... keeps a real live wolf back in his office durin' operatin' hours in case there's ever any trouble from one of the patrons."

Wolfe. Guy closed his eyes. His stomach clenched again, but he wasn't certain why.

"Are you okay, Mr. Jamison?" said Annette, noticing his closed eyes and furrowed forehead.

"Ma ... ddie," managed Guy. He opened his eyes and looked straight at the nurse.

"I'm sorry. What was that?"

"Maddie," he said, more clearly.

"You mean Madeline Walker … Dr. Walker?"

Guy nodded his head yes.

"I'll see if I can find her for you," said Annette. "Bless her heart. She has been in here with you every spare minute, just sitting here and checkin' on you and the day she goes back to her doctoring duties full time, you wake up and need her. You two are good friends from way back, huh?"

Guy nodded.

"I remember her daddy. Boy was he a good doctor. She takes after him, that's a fact.

"I'll go see if I can track her down. Need anything before I set out?"

Guy shook his head no. His neck hurt and he flinched.

"You sure?"

He nodded again. *Please just leave and get Maddie for me.* He suddenly and desperately needed a familiar face. He wanted *her* familiar face. He had to know what was happening.

When Annette left Guy's room, she went immediately to Dr. Ledger.

"He's awake," she said simply, assuming he would know of whom she spoke.

"Uh … great," he muttered caustically under his breath as he finished scribbling notes on a chart. Looking directly at Annette he said, "Let's not make a big deal about this just yet. As soon as it leaks out that our star patient is gracing us with his presence, those hungry reporters will be here again like …"

"Rats on trash?" finished Annette.

"Precisely," said Dr. Ledger, trying to hold back a smile. "Annette, where do you get those?"

"Southern sayings, sir. Pure 'teen southern," said Annette, smiling wide and giving the surgeon a wink. "I'm going to find Maddie at the patient's request."

Dr. Ledger frowned.

"I know, sir. She finally pulls herself away and gets back to some sorta routine today and then he has to go and open his eyes. He seems pretty pitiful and panicked, and she gave strict instructions to find her if he did wake up, so I'm going to do my duty for both parties."

Annette found Maddie exiting the room of a toddler who had stepped in a bed of fire ants in his front yard. Instead of running away, the boy had stood there, paralyzed, until his mother could get to him. Hundreds of the menacing creatures left their marks on his legs and inside his diaper. The bites had triggered an allergic reaction that was almost fatal.

"How's poor sweet baby doin'?" asked Annette.

"He's going to be fine. Just in a lot of pain right now," answered Maddie. "That's the Grover family that just moved here from Asheville. The mother said they don't have fire ants in the mountains. Not a very nice introduction to Wynee is it?"

"No ma'am. I think they would have rather had the pretty welcome basket from the Chamber."

"What's up?" asked Maddie, realizing that Annette was there for more than chit-chat.

"He's awake," said Annette directly.

Maddie dropped her chart and the papers inside slid in every direction on the slick linoleum flooring. She bent to pick up the papers but Annette stopped her.

"You go. I'll get this file back in shape and it will be on your desk."

"Thank you, Annette," said Maddie. She hurried down the hall.

While Guy was alone, he stared intently at the ceiling, trying to decipher what was real and what might have been a dream. He was afraid to close his eyes again for fear of drifting off and missing Maddie. He needed to know what happened to him. His mind slowly began to piece together a mosaic from scattered sundry shards ... Maddie's anger ... the wolf ... the black sofa ... his mother's scream ... the paramedic's voice ... "they're dead!" ...

Maddie entered Guy's room abruptly. "Guy."

He turned his frightened gaze toward her.

Maddie walked to him and put her hand on his arm.

"Guy. It's so good to see you alert."

"Are they dead, Maddie?" he managed, his mouth still cotton. "Are ... my parents ... really dead?" he asked slowly, pleadingly. "What's happened, Maddie? Please tell me what's happened."

"Yes, Guy, your parents are dead."

TEN

ON THE DAY Guy reentered Maddie's life, a catbird sang impatiently at 4:30, long before light penetrated a hovering fog. Maddie woke to the bird's convoluted, boisterous melody. Restless to regain sleep, she eventually gave up an hour later, pulled on running shorts and a t-shirt, stretched for 15, and then jogged the quarter mile to Seabring Dock, turned right, and ran directly down the boardwalk along the rear of the downtown shops. At the end of the boardwalk was a small tidal marsh. The emerging sun backlit the scene and she watched for a moment as snowy egrets – shrouded in the lingering vapor – staked out their fishing territories.

Back at home, she showered, pulled her hair into a smooth, thick ponytail, drank a cup of black tea, and ate a bowl of strawberries and a piece of toast. She then drove to the hospital.

She arrived close to 7:00. Before she entered her small office, she checked on patients. A 52-year-old man had shattered his hip and some bones in his hand after falling off a ladder. A young woman with chronic asthma was in for pneumonia. A teenage boy showing off on his jet ski had crashed into the side of an anchored boat; his right side took the blow.

By 7:49, she was sitting at her desk. Maddie glanced first at the pink note sitting atop her charts. Charlene had called at 7:30 and left a message that she had something for Maddie at her house. *"Please stop by after work. You can plan to have supper with us if you would like,"* the note read.

Maddie looked at her calendar. Wednesday. The Buttses were expecting their son sometime Friday. The parade was set for Saturday morning. It would be fine to stop by.

When she received the official news that Guy would actually grace Wynee with his famous presence, Maddie wrestled. Irritation, doubt, and despondency resulted in little rest. She thought of their oblivious, youthful innocence. They had solidified a joyous bond amid the pall of their parents' blunders. Yet, while the Buttses chose to recognize and eventually welcome the friendship, her own father remained hardened. Maddie surmised that her father died imputing a harsh God who first took his wife and then allowed his only child to seek companionship with the son of the man indirectly responsible for his spouse's death.

Maddie thought of these things and of playing in marshes. She thought of the ice cream truck blaring "The Candy Man" tune and the two of them sitting on the curb racing to see who would get to the bottom of the cone first and find the gumball. What color would it be? She remembered laughing so hard at Guy's rendition of Johnny Quest that she fell off of a swing. She recalled catching six crabs to Guy's one and Mater's two, and watching them fuss and fume and try to figure out what she did differently. There was seldom a memory of her childhood without Guy's presence.

Maddie revisited the volumes of her youth in the weeks prior to Guy's arrival in the town he abandoned almost a decade earlier.

He had not called her directly to tell her he was coming. Random contact with her had ceased with the distance of time. In his express flight to fame, he severed their bond. Their former closeness, she decided, would forever be a pleasant memory. They had explored youth together – as dedicated friends.

At his homecoming, Maddie determined she would meet him with the warmth of an old friend – nothing more. She would keep a safe distance from the hoopla; stay busy at the hospital. She anticipated a speedy entrance and exit resplendent with small town fanfare. Then he would be gone, again. She would continue her life and release any semblance of a grip on the past.

"Got any plans this evening?" asked Stu, popping his head into her office.

Maddie still held the note with Charlene's invitation in her hand. She looked at the note and then at Stu. "The Buttses have asked me to stop by. Can we maybe get together later, when I leave there?"

"Possibly," he said, winking at her. "They probably want to get you involved in the excitement of their son's homecoming," he added. "You *are* going to see Mr. Movie Star while he's here, aren't you?" he asked, fishing.

"I have to work," she answered. "I'm sure I'll run into him and say hello at some point, but …" She looked down at the note again and then back at Stu. "It's really no big deal. Everyone is making way too much out of this whole thing."

"That's all everyone is talking about," agreed Stu. "The girls in the deli earlier were squealing, 'Did you see him in such and such? Oh, yea, he was a *babe* in that!' " he added, conveying the conversation in a high-pitched feminine voice.

Maddie smiled.

"You aren't going down to the parade route on Saturday with those girls to hold an 'OUR GUY'S GREAT!' sign and scream at the top of your lungs?" he said, taunting her.

At this, Maddie reddened slightly. "Go harass someone else. I have charts to finish. I'll call you later."

Stu walked to her desk, leaned over, and kissed her cheek. "Sorry. Didn't mean to hit a nerve."

"You didn't," she said, forcing a smile. "I'll talk to you later."

"See ya!" said Stu cheerfully as he exited her office.

Maddie crumbled up the note and tossed it into the trash can. She turned back toward her charts, intent on concentrating on the day ahead of her.

Around 6 p.m., she was hanging up her lab coat in the locker marked "Dr. Madeline Walker". She dabbed some powder from a Mary Kay compact on her shiny forehead and nose, applied some pale pink lip gloss, and ran a brush through her hair. It was her mother's hair. Everyone said so. Thick, and parted naturally just to the side by an understated cowlick a fainter blond than the rest of her hair, it framed softly the features her father gifted to her: bright gray-green eyes and dimpled cheeks that maintained a slight blush.

Maddie drove the short distance to the Butts's home. She parked on the curb in front of the house and walked down the long driveway to the back entrance. No one, except Charlene's catering clients, ever used the front door. Despite the extraordinary landscaping, wide marble stairs led to an entryway that intimidated true friends, yet impressed strangers. Majestic columns flanked a double, solid mahogany door with beveled glass sidelights and an elaborate transom. The back entrance, through an add-on bead board mud porch that led to the large kitchen, was as simple as the front of the house was grand. Maddie never entered through the front doors.

Smiling, as she walked past new additions to Charlene's yard artistry – mosaic garden stones made from old dinner-ware – she almost missed the rear of the sports car protruding slightly from the Butts's carport. She noticed it just as she was beginning to climb the few steps to the mudroom door. She backed down the steps and walked over to the car.

Yes, it was a rental. Instantly, she felt her heart rate elevate and nausea clutch her. She leaned her back against the car's driver's side door, closed her eyes, and took a deep breath. *Okay, Maddie, pull it together. This is not a big deal. I eat with them. We talk. I leave. No big deal.*

When she opened her eyes, Guy was standing in front of her smiling.

"Zipp …" he said.

Without warning, a sob burst from her like a blast from a trumpet. Her hands flew to her mouth, and she tried to stifle the embarrassing flood, but it would not stop.

"Maddie … Maddie … I'm …" Guy reached out to her, but she drew away. It was the second time in less than a 48-hour period that he had made a woman cry.

Without thinking, Maddie opened the door of the car, climbed in, and locked the door to him. She hid her face in her hands, grasping for composure. She wanted to drive her humiliation into the dark waters of Wynee's bay and vanish.

"Maddie, I'm sorry," said Guy. He had quickly worked his way around to the passenger side and opened the door. He climbed in beside her and put his hand on her shoulder.

For several minutes, she cried into her hands. She breathed deeply and willed herself to stop, but her tear ducts were a separate entity – raw and transparent. They would not close and cut off the flow of water that streamed through her fingers.

Unexpectedly, a momentary flood of hatred engulfed her. The anger that rose up in her stifled her tears, but the shame of her emotional display instantly deflated her. She was spent. In a daze, she gushed, "I'm sorry. This is ridiculous. I need to go. I don't hate you. I should hate you and your parents, but I don't."

"What do you mean, Maddie? I know I've been a terrible, terrible friend. But my parents? They've always loved you like a daughter. I'm the prodigal son. They should hate me for my selfishness."

He rubbed her shoulder and then said, "I just got so caught up in it. It's impossible not to. I'm sorry I haven't been a friend to you, Maddie, truly I am."

Then, with that same teasing, boyish playfulness she had known years ago, he added, "You forgive me, don't you, Zipp?"

"Don't call me that!" she yelled at him. "You have no right to call me that!"

She climbed out of the car and slammed the door. "Tell your parents I'm sorry about dinner!" Wanting to run, she instead walked forcefully down the driveway toward her car.

"Maddie … wait!" shouted Guy, running up behind her. He grabbed her arm just as she was reaching for the car door. "Maddie, don't run off like this. I'm sorry that I've upset you so much."

"I just didn't realize how seeing you would affect me, Guy. I'm the one who's sorry. I should have dealt with losing your friendship a long time ago, but I guess I haven't. I just need some time to think about what I'm feeling."

Suddenly struck with the fact that he was at the road, exposed, he looked around to see if anyone – neighbors, passing cars – recognized him. His mind flashed a scene of Wynee's residents mobbing him there in front of his house.

"Unbelievable," said Maddie, shaking her head and pulling free from his grasp. "Better run inside before your fans see that you're already here!" She got inside her car, pulled the door closed, and drove away with Guy standing solemnly on the curb.

Guy's self-absorbed thoughts sobered her. The deluge from her eyes ceased. Her body stiffened. She was angry – at herself and at Guy. She drove the short distance home in a rush and hurried inside. She immediately dashed upstairs and stripped off her clothes. She felt dirty and wanted to wash away the embarrassment of her actions, the shame of exposing her emotions to someone she no longer knew or cared to know.

I can't believe I got so upset. I can't believe I got so upset. Her mind played the words over and over again. As she showered, she wondered if her mother had felt the same distress years ago – distress that led to her death. *Like mother, like daughter. Like father like son. Did Lawrence have that same self-absorbed spirit? Before his conversion?*

Maddie knew Lawrence only as a loving, giving, and righteous person … a man who walked the line. Had she known him before – before her relationship with his son became like breathing in and out every day – would she have liked him?

When Squash had eventually revealed to her the reason for her mother's death, she dared not believe her. Not Lawrence, the hapless teddy bear of a man who was unabashedly accepting of his wife's quirky ways. A Jacob of a father to his only son. Not Lawrence.

But somehow she did know it was Lawrence. Had she sensed all along, just beneath her skin, that it was Lawrence?

It explained the dynamics of the Butts family and the distressed disposition of her own father.

"It's been in me to tell ya for a long time, child," Squash had said to her when she was home in between her sophomore and junior year at USC. "Now that your daddy's done gone, it's time you know the truth about the Buttses … and why your daddy got so disturbed by your takin' up a friendship with Guy. He had his reason, child. He had his reason."

Maddie believed that Lawrence's kindness toward and acceptance of her was atonement for his sin. And Charlene had nurtured her for the same reason: to make amends for her husband's sin, and to be a motherly influence on a girl who had no mother.

Maddie had every reason to hate the Buttses after what Squash told her … after learning the real reason her mother lived only long enough to enjoy her daughter's first few months of life. But she didn't hate them. They, and the faith they led her to, provided the warm blanket she needed for her soul.

She had no knowledge of her mother's personality, but she surmised that it was probably similar to her own. Maddie dealt with stressful situations in a calm, level-headed manner – to a point. Then, instead of a gathering build-up to an emotional episode, the feelings would just surge forth and scatter like birdshot out of a shotgun. No more keeping it under wraps. Squash often exclaimed, "Now if that ain't your mamma all over," when Maddie pitched a fit as a child.

Before she even returned to USC that fall, Maddie had forgiven Lawrence. She would not tell the Buttses she knew. It would only serve to disrupt the hard scab that formed over the situation. *Alea iacta est*, she recalled from her Latin class at USC. The die is cast.

But Lawrence had to have been an egocentric when he pursued her mother so ardently and carelessly. This was a personality trait, she judged, that was genetically passed onto his son even while Lawrence, himself, had allowed it to flow from him that baptismal day into the waters of Conversion Creek.

The sky was darkening when Maddie stepped out of the shower. She felt somewhat better, though her eyes burned from crying. Her head ached. The phone was ringing, but she ignored it. Probably Guy. In her bathrobe, she made her way downstairs and filled a kettle with water. Hot tea always soothed her. Squash had taught her to float a spearmint leaf in a cup of Earl Grey just to give it a tinge of flavor. "Better'n' sugar, I think," Squash would tell her.

The phone rang again. Maddie sat at the kitchen table and stared blankly forward. She sipped her tea calmly, imagining the warm fluid penetrating and relaxing every muscle. The phone rang again, and then Maddie heard a helicopter overhead.

Maybe there is a trauma at the hospital. A small landing pad had been poured on a vacant lot next to the hospital to accept a medical chopper if necessary. She checked her beeper on the kitchen counter to make certain it was working. It was. She decided to call the hospital just to check. Doreen, who typically worked day shifts at the hospital's Welcome Desk, answered.

"No, nothing big going on here," she informed Maddie. Then Maddie got an earful about why Doreen had to work a double shift.

She hung up the phone; it immediately rang again. She let it ring. She knew it must be Guy. Maddie had no answering machine. She felt like her beeper served her important needs. Since she had been absorbed in Guy as a child, and then in her work at the hospital after residency, she had few friends who needed to reach her. The Buttses called her at work. She sometimes was invited to Mater's to dine with his family. She had become friends, of late, with Trisha in radiology. They occasionally managed a walk through town and by the marsh if they both happened to finish at the hospital at the same time. And then there was Stu, whom she saw every day – work related or otherwise.

Stu! She remembered she was supposed to call him. Maybe he was trying to call her. She picked up the phone and dialed his number. He answered immediately.

"Have you tried to call me?" she asked.

"Yes, a few minutes ago. Have you been home long?"

"For a short while. Did you call more than once?"

"No. Why?"

"Oh, no reason."

"Were you at the Buttses when the ants invaded?" said Stu, with a sarcastic laugh.

"What are you talking about?" asked Maddie.

"The reporters! Movie Man must already be here – or they're hoping to catch him pulling in. When I drove by after work there were at least half a dozen cars and vans parked along the road and a helicopter was hovering overhead. I think sleepy little Wynee is going to get a rude awakening!"

"I learned that the reason Charlene asked me over for dinner was to surprise me with Guy's early arrival," Maddie told him. She decided just to lay it all out for him, matter-of-factly. "Guy was my dearest friend for a long time. But he decided that friendship was no longer important the minute he stepped his foot away from this place, and I'm not real interested in pretending we're still buddy-buddy. He was there, and I didn't behave too well, and now I'm home."

She felt relief the minute she said the word, "home." Her home, the home that raised her and was left to her by her father, provided great solace.

"I just want to rest tonight, Stu. I'd love to get together with you another night. Maybe this weekend? Can we do that?"

There was a pause.

"Of course. No problem. I kind of just wanted to park across the street from the Butts's place and watch the action tonight anyway," he said, teasingly.

"Stu!"

"Kidding."

After a pause, Stu said, "Maddie."

"Yes."

"Is it more than just a broken friendship you're dealing with?"

After a silent moment, Maddie offered, "Yes … uh probably … yes. But not what you might be thinking."

"Do you want to talk about it more tonight?"

"Sometime … but not tonight."

"No problem. I'll see you tomorrow. Pleasant dreams."

Maddie refilled her tea cup with steaming water and returned the partially-used tea bag to the cup. She did not like her tea too strong and found that she could get three, sometimes four cups from the same bag before the drink tasted only of minty hot water.

It was still fairly early and she felt like sleep would elude her if she tried to retire. Instead, she pulled a book off the shelf, *Cold Mountain*. She wanted her mind away from Wynee. Reading for fun was a luxury. She read charts and medical journals daily. She was often too tired to read anything in her spare time. It had taken her almost a year to read midway through *Cold Mountain*.

Maddie was admiring Frazier's poetry of words in a reference to the North Carolina mountains when she thought she heard a knock at the back door. She waited a moment. She heard it again. It was just a little more than a tap, but the sound was slightly louder the second time.

Hesitantly, she made her way to the back door. Standing there, forlorn, was Guy.

"I come to make peace, Kee-mo-sabi," he said, sheepishly, as Maddie cracked open the screen door. "You have pierced Tonto's heart with arrow."

"You just don't get it, do you?" said Maddie. Raising her voice, she added, "It's not about the movies or television or you! It's about having some consideration for the people that are supposed to be a part of your life. Namely, your parents. If you didn't want to maintain our friendship because I'm just a girl you grew up with in a podunk little southern town and it doesn't fit with your glamorous image, that's fine. But your parents! Come on, Guy. It's not like they beat you or anything. They're a little quirky, but they're your parents. People understand. They don't label you because of who your parents are. It would not have tarnished your reputation to call and visit your own parents now and then."

"Can I ...?"

Her frustration level escalated with every sentence that tumbled out. She suddenly wanted to pierce his ears with the resentment that had grown surreptitiously inside her. "I don't have either of my parents living, and yet you have two loving, healthy, faithful parents whom you have basically ignored for years!"

"Maddie," managed Guy in between her breaths, "I did want to apologize to you for not attending your father's funeral. I was in Indonesia at the time filming ..."

"I don't give a da…" She composed herself. "I don't care that you didn't attend my father's funeral. You were the last person I expected to be there or to even hear from. I'm glad for your success, Guy. Truly, I am. It's what you always wanted. And the reason your parents aren't so hard on you about ignoring them is because they know it's what they always wanted as well. But it came at a price. You traded – completely and wholeheartedly – your relationships here for fame. We had a wonderful, sweet childhood and a friendship, once. For some reason – something only God could have cooked up – we were brought together. And it resulted in as much restoration as could take place in your parents …"

"What do you mean?"

Maddie could not stave off the verbal tide long enough for Guy to speak. She was afraid she would not finish saying all that rapidly whirled within her.

"Our friendship also meant that I got to learn about God and to have two people in my life that have been as close to parents as I'll have from here on out. But as far as our friendship, it's done. We can't go back. We were as tight as people could get – back then. You knew everything about me there is to know about a person. But you know *nothing* about me now."

She glared at him before finishing.

"That has been your choice, and I just need for you to leave me alone while you're here."

"Maddie, you're killing me here," said Guy, visibly struck by her words. "I made a mistake by not keeping in touch … a terrible mistake. I just got on the ride out there and I didn't get off. I apologized to my parents about that. I came over here to apologize to you. I love you, Maddie. I've always loved you."

"Empty! *Empty!*" yelled Maddie. "It's all empty, Guy. It means nothing!" She slammed the door in his face and turned back into her house. Tears streamed down her face.

Guy followed her in and grabbed her arm. "Maddie, don't do this."

"I will not let you come here and act like everything's fine and then not see or hear from you again for years. I can't take that, Guy! And I'm begging you right now: *Do not* do that to your parents!"

"I won't Maddie, I promise. I had no idea it affected you this badly. I'm going to juggle things better, you'll see. I want us to start over. I was hoping for a better reunion with you than this."

"Just pick up where we left off? It doesn't work like that, Guy. This isn't a movie. There are *real* feelings involved, not pretend ones."

Maddie pulled her arm from him and said, half facing him, "I hope you receive all the praise and adulation you deserve while you're here in Wynee. And I hope you have a good life. I sincerely do. The friendship we had will always be precious to me, Guy, but I'm just not interested in trying to create a new friendship that will quickly disappear the minute you're distracted."

The whir of a helicopter intensified momentarily as it flew over Maddie's home, causing Guy to stare toward the ceiling. The loud humming of the propeller grew fainter as it flew into the distance. Guy listened for it as it faded away.

"Oh, they'll be back tomorrow. Don't you worry," said Maddie, scornfully.

"Maddie, please …"

"Good night, Guy." Maddie turned her back toward him. He stood just inside the kitchen door. She turned off the light, leaving him in the dark, and walked upstairs.

For several moments, there were no sounds. Maddie's muscles tightened wondering if he would follow her upstairs, or stand in her kitchen all night waiting for the morning. Then Maddie heard him feel around for her phone. She heard him say quietly, "Just turn on the front porch light and walk out onto the porch like you're going to say something to them. I'll sneak in the back door."

She heard the sound of a door closing, and she knew he was gone.

ELEVEN

With the word "dead," Guy turned his battered face away from Maddie. He stared out the window and fixed his eyes on a shaft of sunlight broken free from the bondage of a dark, ominous-looking cloud.

Maddie allowed him to stay that way for several moments before speaking. "Guy …"

When he did not respond, she touched his hand. He flinched as if in pain. "Guy …"

She heard a mumbled whisper and walked around to the other side of the bed. She sat down on a chair so that her face was at eye-level with his.

"I don't remember what happened," he whispered again. A tear formed in his still-swollen left eye, drifted down his bruised cheek, and disappeared onto the pillow. "I don't re-member … please tell me. How did they die?"

It began to rain outside. Natural illumination disappeared.

"Are you sure you want to hear this right now, Guy? You've been in and out of consciousness, but mostly out, for a while now. You should just …"

"I want … to know … what I did," he said, louder. Another tear spilled, and Guy took a deep breath, closed his eyes, and tried to stifle his emotions.

Maddie waited.

When he opened his eyes again he said, "I'm ready."

After Maddie told him about how she became upset at seeing him and how he called his home that night and then left hers, Guy closed his eyes and drifted off – momentarily. He opened his eyes and looked at Maddie.

"You never showed up at your parents' house, Guy," she said.

He closed his eyes again. Grainy images projected slowly and repulsively in his head. The dark room images lightened and became forms.

"You want me to stop for now?" asked Maddie.

He opened his eyes and nodded his head. He closed his eyes again.

But with his eyes closed, the pictures gradually became clearer and the details filled in like sand flowing into crevices. He saw himself, crouched in the bushes behind the only house he knew as home. He heard the muffled conversations of reporters gathered at the front door. He remembered feeling sick. He felt the weight of Maddie's words … her emotions. *Why the hell did I think coming back to Wynee was a good idea?*

Inside his house, Guy knew it would be much of the same. An interrogation would ensue. "Where's Maddie? Is she okay? What happened? She seemed pretty upset, Guy."

He had looked at the aging, antebellum abode once more and then turned away from it. He walked away from his home and the reporters and into the darkness.

Guy recalled desperately needing a drink. *Something harder than beer.* He snuck through the camellia hedges along the back of his parents' neighbors, the Poteats. He squirreled along a picket fence and scurried down a dirt lane behind a row of clapboard houses. Dogs barked and a sensor spotlighted movement in the yard; he dodged into the shadows and crept away.

Guy knew every square inch of Wynee. It came back to him as if the past years were only a flicker and he was 10 again, or 12, or 14 – running to meet Maddie. He made his way around the gravestones at Emmanuel Methodist Church. When he was 13, the church burned to the ground. Guy stood and looked at the illuminated building, an exact replica of the former structure, and imagined the heat from the tremendous blaze he had watched in awe with Maddie statue-like by his side. A safe distance away from the firetrucks and hoses, the two companions had remained, side by side, without saying a word until there was nothing but a marble pulpit rising soot-stained but intact from a pile of black ash. On the way to their own church that next Sunday morning, Charlene gasped and Lawrence stopped the car in reverence: the congregation of Emmanuel Methodist Church gathered in prayer among the charred ruins. The pastor laid his Bible on the soiled white pulpit as they pulled slowly away. Women's voices in song drifted above the debris.

Guy exited the graveyard and worked his way to the fringes of Wynee. It did not take long. There were plenty of juke joint shacks on the outskirts of town before he left. Surely there would still be at least one that would serve him a drink. *Shouldn't be too crowded this early.*

He meandered the pathway to Marshy Cove. A deluge of memories engulfed him, and he paused to imagine Maddie, and sometimes Mater, squishing down the always-wet, narrow path flanked by prickly marsh grass. Laughing and teasing about the threat of snakes grabbing at their ankles, they walked quickly and purposefully until reaching a hidden, rickety wooden rowboat they had found, patched, and hidden in a grove of wild fan palms. Often they fished or captured crabs. But the picture of them venturing to Shine Island pierced Guy at that particular moment. It was one of those perfect childhood recollections that captures the essence of what it is to be young and untroubled by the world.

Shine Island was so named because local moonshiners mixed spirits there during Prohibition. Only a half mile wide and a quarter mile deep, it was uninhabitable because of the dense marsh surrounding it. It was only accessible by boats small enough to maneuver through the marsh grasses at high tide and thus became an ideal still sight for the production of illegal corn liquor.

When the stills that made what pious townspeople called "the devil's drink" were cleared away, an interesting phenomenon transpired. Each June thereafter, purple martins roosted on Shine Island. For a few years, not enough of the birds flocked there for Wyneeans to take much notice. Then they came by the hundreds, then thousands. Around 7:30 each summer evening, birds that spent the day clearing insects from around the homes of Wynee, sped toward Shine Island as if a gravitational pull simultaneously drew them there. Some folks religiously situated themselves on the benches occupying Wynee's riverwalk to witness the "miracle" of the bird swarms flitting and gliding anxiously toward the island.

"Them birds have taken a 'shine' to that island," one resident quipped.

For observers in downtown Wynee, the sight was a blending of small black dots forming an ashen cloud over the island. The feathered vortex twirled for a few moments and then spread out – a thick black carpet descending over trees and then waving up again. By 8:00, the skies cleared and the birds rested in the tangle of sea myrtles prevalent on the island. Dawn prompted the birds to make their pilgrimage back to the far corners of Wynee. The spectacle happened again and again until mid-September when the martins felt an internal tug toward their South American winter home.

As spectacular as the gathering of the birds was to towns-folk viewing it from a distance, it was unlike anything else up close. Guy summoned the experience as he stood alone in the darkness.

It was a summer ritual to row the boat just a few feet from the shores of Shine Island and wait for the birds. While they waited, Guy taunted Maddie by tilting the boat from side to side to scare her into thinking he would capsize it. They splashed one another and chortled loudly at his obnoxious attempts at joke telling. When the birds began soaring overhead, silence ensued. No one said, "Hush" or "Quiet" or "Shut up!" The gracefulness of the birds above them and their merging together in unison was enough to still them.

They lounged in the boat reveling in the astonishing chorus of a lilting melody and the deafening effect of wings flapping in unison.

It was over as swiftly as it had begun. No one spoke for many minutes after the cloak of birds submerged into the trees. Maddie sat up – tears on her face – and said, "That's God."

It pained him to remember. He needed that drink.

He moved on in the darkness, finding a back road into the countryside. It was a Thursday night. Few cars passed Guy, who kept as far off the shoulder as possible. Wynee people, for the most part, were stay-inners in the evenings. He did not expect much activity. Still, he thought how irritated he might be if he called attention to himself. His step quickened. He wanted to find a place and hide.

He thought there was a lowly drinking shack on the fringes of town rumored to be run by a man with a pet wolf. Guy vaguely recalled his father meeting the man through his magistrate duties and conveying some details of eccentricities during a family meal the summer before Guy departed to Hollywood.

Guy spotted a lone illumination intruding in the darkness. He walked toward it. With every step, introspection bared down, about Maddie, his parents, his career, his past. He needed that drink to desensitize him. Tomorrow would be better, he thought. *His mercies are new every morning.*

"No!" said Guy aloud into the black.

He wanted his mind empty. *Isn't that what Maddie had said to me? Empty! Empty!*

Irritation rising, Guy's steps hastened.

As he drew nearer to the light, he made out a few cars parked in front of a structure. The way the cars were parked, parallel to one another along the entrance, he ascertained that it was not a residence. His eyes adjusted to bold lettering painted onto a sheet of plywood: Wolfe's Crabbs, Beear, and Careeokee. Guy smirked and shook his head. The sign was attached to two junk cars piled one on top of another. Inside the windowless cars were miscellaneous beer bottles and cans. Attached to the hood of the bottom car were hundreds of pieces of old chewing gum that formed a fairly large "W."

"Nice," whispered Guy.

Instead of being a wooden shack, the establishment was a drab double-wide trailer that had seen better days. Concrete steps led to the door, and the windows were painted over black from the outside.

Guy planted his foot firmly onto the first step and hesitated. He did not know why then, but he would contemplate that pause over and over again later. He took the two additional steps that changed his life.

Evening was fully upon Wolfe's when Guy entered through its metal door. Guy recognized immediately that the lounge attracted not Wynee's finest, but rather its misshapen and fully warted members. Guy noticed a varied lot congregated around the bar area. Four pot-bellied bikers – obvious in black leather and tattoos; two stout black men in do-rags leaning on the opposite end of the bar; and, directly in the middle of the bar speaking to the bartender was an elderly, weathered man who looked, to Guy, like a modern-day sea captain. He was laughing out of one side of his mouth.

The identity of Wolfe was apparent due to the large wolf-head tattoo advertised on his fairly exposed chest. The proprietor wore a shirt, but it was missing buttons.

As Guy positioned himself closest to the aging stroke victim, all eyes studied him momentarily. Used to stares, he waited for recognition. Interest was fleeting, and they resumed drinking and conversations. Guy leaned onto the bar as Wolfe finished telling the older man what sounded like a fishing tale. A gray/black face of fur and two steely eyes stared back at Guy from just below the bartender's waist. A low growl formed in the wolf's throat.

"Whoa, boy," said Wolfe. "You know you ain't supposed to get testy with our guests." He thumped the animal on the ear. The wolf dropped to the ground submissively.

"Guess that's why they call you Wolfe," said Guy, nervously.

"Nope. Call me Wolfe 'cause my name's Wolfe. What you havin'?"

"A shot of Jack, and keep them coming," said Guy.

"Can't read?" asked Wolf.

"Huh?"

"It states very clearly on my sign that we serve beer. And if you want something to eat there's crabs. And if you want to sing, there's karaoke."

"Don't you have anything stronger?" He didn't want to aggravate a man with a wolf at his feet, but he knew it would take a whole lot of beers to do any immediate numbing. He wanted full-out, fast relief from the day's pressures.

"Depends on who you are. You ain't a regular and I'm thinkin' you're not from around here."

Guy could feel the eyes of the other patrons on him again.

"I was born in Wynee. Just haven't wanted a drink enough to visit your establishment before."

"What's your name?" asked the haggard man next to Guy.

Wolfe leaned onto the counter equally anticipating the answer.

"Rhett Butts," said Guy, suddenly thankful his parents had been generous with names.

"Red Butts!" screamed one of the bikers. A roar of laughter filled the fabricated building.

"Rhett … I said Rhett," said Guy loudly, but the others were enjoying the humorous moment. Irritated, he demanded, "Just give me a beer … two of them to start."

"Come with me, son!" said Wolfe, commandingly.

The laughter ceased.

The animal rose and sauntered beside its master as Wolfe motioned Guy to a back room.

"Nevermind!" said Guy, backing toward the door.

"No really, *come here*," said Wolfe. He walked from behind the counter and was upon Guy in only a few steps. He put his arm around Guy, forcefully, smiling at him. The wolf eyed Guy suspiciously and sniffed his legs. "Just want to have a friendly chat. Really."

Wolfe led Guy to a room behind the bar area and shut the door.

"I'm not looking for any trouble," said Guy. "I'll just leave."

"No reason to leave, Mr. Movie Star. Yeah, I know who you are. Your daddy's had some dealins' with me in the past. He was right fair with me. And I've seen a few of your flicks. Pretty good. I just wanted to make sure you ain't no Federal guy lookin' to bust me for liquor. What you in here for? Researchin' for a movie?"

Guy felt the beads of perspiration form on his brow, but he thought that wiping them off in front of Wolfe would expose apprehension.

"No. I'm not researching. I just need a drink."

"Well I've got a drink for you. It's a drink all right, heh, if ya know what I mean." He winked at Guy. He handed him a cloudy glass and poured some clear liquid into it. Guy hesitated. He wished he had not opened his mouth and just ordered a beer like the rest of the patrons. Wolfe stared at him, waiting for him to take the drink. He drank it down in one long gulp. Immediately, his breath left him and his throat burned. He put his hand onto the back of a nearby chair to steady himself.

"Whoa!" exclaimed Guy. "Now that's some mean stuff," he added, thankful to be breathing again. "Give me one more shot of that, and beer will do me for a while. Is that your own brew?"

"Could be," said Wolfe. "It's going to cost you, but I know you can afford it. Just don't make out that you got anything but beer in here tonight, you hear? You understanding me?" He patted his wolf on the head for emphasis.

"Fine."

"Or else," Wolfe added, smiling, "my dog Freddy here might get a bit testy."

"That's a dog?"

"To you and to everyone else it's a dog," said Wolfe, winking again. "Just like to you and everyone else you're only drinkin' beer tonight. Now, since I'm serving you *only beer* tonight, I'll need a $40 deposit to start you a tab. Any problem with that?"

"None," said Guy, pulling two $20 bills from his wallet. As soon as the money rested in Wolfe's large palm, his other hand opened the door, releasing Guy.

He situated himself on a barstool next to the sea captain, who turned toward him with a crooked grin. Guy noticed that few teeth were involved in his attempted smile.

"What do you think I do for a livin', young man? Can you guess?"

"You're a fisherman and you have your own boat?"

"Give this man here a drink!" said the old man, poking Guy in the ribs. "Amazing! How did you know that?"

"Well, I … uh … study people's characters for a living," said Guy, carefully.

"You one of those psychologists?"

"Something like that." Guy looked at Wolfe, who glanced at him and winked while tapping his beer.

Guy took a giant gulp. The response to the bubbly liquid on his already scorched throat forced an immediate cough to heave from his chest. The old man whacked him on the back.

"You okay?"

"Yeah," said Guy, catching his breath. "Guess it went down the wrong pipe."

Guy sipped the beers slowly after that, allowing his esophagus to adjust to the fiery sensation. Once the liquid made its way into his stomach, however, the feeling was that of satin and silk. The salve mollified his body and his mind.

He gulped the next one and settled in for a third.

A few more visitors trickled into Wolfe's. Women who joined the bikers, and a stout balding man with a grimy t-shirt sat in one corner. Wolfe poured the dirty man a beer and plunked it in front of him indifferently.

Guy said little. He slumped over his drink, enjoying the sedative effects. Insolence, often the product of inebriation from a hard, homemade brew, goaded Guy to gradually turn and eye the squat, middle-aged man in the corner. He recognized him. He was not certain at first, but then it came to him – even in his premature stupor.

Guy stood up and walked directly over to the man, pulled out a chair, and sat down. Unshaven, with motor-oil stained hands, the man's eyes widened and his pupils bulged white from his sockets.

"What the hell do you think you're doin'?" he boomed at Guy.

"Just came over for a friendly chat," slurred Guy.

"Not feelin' friendly."

"I know you."

"What?" The man pushed his chair back and stood up. He was a good foot shorter than Guy, but wide and muscular.

"You're Timmy's father," said Guy. "You're the one that gave Timmy his nice facial features when he was a kid."

"Why you …" The man drew back his fist, but Wolfe was already there pushing him back down into his chair.

"Sit, Bud," said Wolfe. "Don't start anything."

"Just having a friendly chat," said Guy, smiling cockily, standing back up. "He must not be feeling too friendly."

"You come back over to the bar and behave yourself," said Wolfe. "We'll be starting our 'Oke Off' soon. You can get yourself a number and sing all your troubles away."

"Do you know what that man did?" said Guy, leaning into Wolfe carelessly.

"I know. I know."

Ignoring Wolfe, Guy said, "He rearranged little Timmy's face. Timmy was a classmate of mine in grade school. Timmy never could come back to school after that. His dad made him a freak!" Guy said the word *freak* loudly, garnering the attention of his bar mates. "When they asked Daddy over there what happened to his boy, he told them Timmy was just so stupid and clumsy that he fell out of a tree stand onto his face. How do you like that?"

Wolfe sat Guy down firmly onto the barstool and put his large hands on his shoulders. "He did some time for that. But let me tell you something, hotshot, you can drink in my place and I will take your money, but if you push it, you're out! How do you like *that*?"

Guy smiled, "I like that. Bring me another drink."

"I know who that is." Guy heard one of the biker women squeal. She turned her stare in his direction. Guy squinted his eyes. She seemed to have unusually large arms and legs and a thin, straight up and down middle. He looked over, raised his glass, and grinned broadly.

"That's Guy Jamison."

"Who?" asked one of the men.

"You know! The actor! Used to live here! Parade's on Saturday!"

"Big deal," said one of the bikers.

"So what brings you in here?" said the woman with the disproportioned figure. She picked up her barstool and slinked beside Guy. "I've never met a real live movie star before."

"Hey!" said one of the bikers. "You get back here, Roseanne!"

Seeing another fire developing, Wolfe walked quickly to the karaoke stage area, grabbed the microphone, and made the announcement that the 'Oke Off' would begin soon. He ran through the list of contestant rules.

"Eeeee," squealed Roseanne, jumping up from the stool beside Guy. "I'm goin' to win tonight. I can feel it!"

"I can feel it too, honey," said Guy, repugnantly.

"You can, *really*?" said Roseanne, turning to look at Guy. "Will you sign my Wolfe's t-shirt when I do?"

"You bet." Guy saluted her. Turning back to the old man, who was still seated and sitting quietly at the bar, Guy garbled, "Do men salute *you* on your boat, or what? That would be way cool to be saluted."

"You tryin' to get yourself killed tonight?"

"What? I was … asking you about your saloon … salute," said Guy, trying to position his hand once again over his right eye.

"You ain't been in here an hour, son, and you're already too drunk to have any sense. And, believe me, I know drunk. Are you really in the movies?"

"I'm Guy Jamison," he said, curiously lucid. "You've never heard of me? I played Jack Parks in *Jump* about the World War II parachuter. Got an Academy Award nomination for that one. Got to actually jump out of an airplane! Is that impressive or what? I've been in seven feature films so far! That's almost a movie a year. Played Davis Best in …"

"Ain't seen a movie since *Gone with the Wind*," the man interrupted. "Wife made me see that one. Got so stinkin' mad about what Sherman done that I ain't been back to see no movie since. What I'm wonderin' about you, young man, is why you're in here gettin' stewed to the gills drownin' some kinda' sorrow if you're rich and famous?"

The karaoke competition began. The two black guys in do-rags introduced a song from Dean Martin and Jerry Lewis's last musical together – "Hollywood or Bust."

Guy tried to speak. His eyes watered, and he rubbed them both with the palms of his hands, letting them linger there. When he pulled his palms from his eyes, his bar mate was gone. He looked at the stage; the man stood in line, waiting his turn. Guy finished his drink and asked for another.

The fisherman announced his selection, *Let's Get it On*, by Marvin Gaye. Those present roared their approval, the sound bouncing off the flimsy walls. Guy smiled and watched as the man pitifully, but passionately, sang and gyrated his partially debilitated body to the slow, seductive music. The crowd whistled and clapped as the man sauntered confidently back to the bar.

"Wow. You're … prime," said Guy, drunkenly grabbing at a California word. "Maybe … I can, you know, play … uh … a character based on … uh … you in a movie sometime."

"I hope not," said the man. He finished off the beer in front of him, left a bill on the bar, and smiled his half smile at Wolfe. He put his hand on Guy's shoulder and said, "Go home." Then he exited through the trailer's metal door, leaving Roseanne belting out Barbra Streisand's *Evergreen*.

Guy did not budge from his stool. He watched the show, drank his beer, and thought about nothing. His eyes were heavy and moist, and he abruptly felt his bladder's urging.

"Toilet?" he asked Wolfe, who pointed in the direction of the bathroom.

Guy managed to wash his hands and splash water on his face. He looked at his face in the smudged frameless mirror. He observed his image for a few moments, as if he were seeing his reflection for the first time. Loud whistling from beyond the restroom door beckoned him. He opened the door and immediately fixated on the object of the commotion. A woman with a short, form-fitting black dress and black pumps had entered the bar. Her bleached blond hair was teased high in the front, sections cascaded over one eye. She had on black eyeliner and dark eyeshadow. She was on the arm of a tall, brawny, bald man with a thick, disheveled mustache who did not seem to mind – but rather enjoy – the whistles and catcalls.

"Lo-rraine. Lo-rraine. Lo-rraine." The small audience cheered.

Roseanne was back at the bar, her voluminous arms folded in disgust.

"She had to come tonight," said Roseanne to Guy, who sat back down on his stool at the bar. "Thinks she's so hot."

She is, thought Guy.

Lorraine's lips were bright red with a touch of clear gloss. As Guy watched her take the stage, those lips punctured the smoked-filled room. Even in his haze, he regarded those lips. He watched them form the words of the song, *Diamonds are a Girl's Best Friend*, by Marilyn Monroe. He stared while she grabbed the microphone and moved it closer to that scarlet mouth. He enjoyed the movement of that mouth while it seductively expressed the words to the song.

Guy, along with everyone else in the bar, except Roseanne, cheered wildly during Lorraine's performance. Clearly relishing her tawdry fame, she curtsied and then strutted over to the bar from the stage area with the bald man proudly attached to her side.

Lorraine stopped in front of Guy, her mouth open.

"Oh my … Oh … Oh my … hell fire, it isn't? Are you … Are you Guy Jamison? Please tell me you are!!"

"Yes. I am."

"Oh. Oh." Her red lips made a perfect circle when she said the word. "Oh, I can't believe it. I was going to be the first person on the sidewalk on Saturday to see you pass on the street and now, here you are, sitting right smack in front of me!"

Guy was aware of all the attention she directed toward him, but he cared less. The alcohol narcotized all common sense. He considered nothing: his parents, Maddie, Wynee, acting. Just those lips, which were close enough to touch.

"Well, I've just got to get my picture taken with you. And I've just got to get your autograph. Oh my. I just can't believe it," she said, fumbling through a black purse. "Can you believe this, Phil?"

"Can't believe it," said her companion, nonplussed.

Lorraine pulled out a compact disposable camera. She shoved it in Phil's hand and wiggled her way backward until she was leaning against Guy.

"Ohhh! Wait a minute, Phil." She reached back into the purse and pulled out a tube of the brightest red lipstick Guy had ever seen. She flipped up the front flap of her purse, revealing a mirror. Guy watched in the reflection while she slowly added another layer to her already crimson lips.

"Okay. I'm ready," said Lorraine to Phil, who rolled his eyes.

"Come on then, there." He snapped it hurriedly before Lorraine had a chance to pose.

"Phil," she whined. "Honey, I wasn't ready."

She put her arm around Guy and tilted her cheek toward his. Right before Phil snapped the picture, Lorraine puckered her lips. At the same time, a beeper attached to Phil's side made a loud beep and flashed a red light.

"No way!" said Phil, angrily. "Wolfe, can I borrow your phone?" He glared at Guy who was suddenly enveloped by the scant female population inside the bar. Lorraine was closest, asking Guy about his movies. Phil hesitated before moving toward the phone, but then brushed the scene away with a backhanded gesture.

When Phil returned to the bar a moment later, he grabbed Lorraine's arm and tugged her from the tight throng.

"A call came in, I've got to go. *We've* got to go," he said, eyeing Guy.

"I thought you weren't starting until next week!" she answered, annoyed.

"I was, honey, but another guy, Alan, got some kind of stomach bug all of a sudden and they asked me if I'd be on call just in case. You know what happens when there's a full moon. Every Tom, Dick, and Harry wants a ride in an ambulance to the hospital. It's probably nothin' much. We can come back later if it's not too late. Come on! I have to leave right now!"

"Well, I ain't leavin'. I'll get a ride. The decision hasn't been made whether I won the Oke Off or not."

"You won, sweetheart. Hands down. Now come on."

"I ain't goin'. Besides, when will I ever get to sit and talk with a real live movie star again? Sherry and Rhonda will be 20 shades of red when they hear!"

"I can't argue with you any longer," said Phil. "I have to go!" With a glare in Guy's direction, he marched to the trailer door, opened it, and turned, half expecting to see Lorraine walking after him. She was, instead, pushing her way back into the prime position next to Guy.

Nursing yet another beer, Guy saw the red lips through a mist, returning to him. The bald head did not accompany them.

Guy sloppily signed a few napkins and shirtsleeves and mentioned his Academy Award nomination more than once. When Lorraine was crowned champion of Oke Off, he signed his name large across the entire back side of the t-shirt

– above the wolf's head. The signature was juvenile, barely legible.

The initial 40-proof liquid took hold of Guy's limbs first and then deadened his mind. The beers did their work to stupefy discernment. Guy found himself alone with those tempting lips. The beers – too many to count – entitled him to partake in that redness.

"Let's move it on over here," Guy said to Lorraine, grabbing her hand and leading her, staggeringly, to a black patent leather sofa with stitching deteriorating from around the arms. He had seen the sofa in a shadowy niche when he made his way to the bathroom earlier. It was just slightly out of view of Wolfe's other guests.

Before they were fully situated onto the dank seating, Guy plunged toward her slovenly and copiously planted his mouth on hers. She accepted it, gladly. Yet, there was no lingering on those lips or further advancements as Guy's head leaned listlessly to the side and flopped onto her shoulder. A red smear trailed from her mouth to her chin.

Lorraine pushed him off of her shoulder, and his body flopped onto the sofa. Guy was smiling and slurring his words. Without moving or heaving forward, he vomited a flood of beer and moonshine down the front of his shirt and onto the fake leather.

"Ewww. Wolfe!!! Ewww!" screeched Lorraine. She jumped up from the sofa and met Wolfe, who roared obscenities.

"Get him out of my place!" said Wolfe, to everyone and anyone still left inside. He grabbed a wad of bar towels from behind the counter and threw them onto the front of Guy.

Two of the bikers, still hanging around, stood up as volunteers. They grabbed Guy by his two unsoiled arms and dragged him, mumbling, out the door and down the concrete steps. They dumped him in a heap next to the stacked junk cars.

Unabashedly, Guy curled into a fetal position and slumbered vacantly. Patrons leaving Wolfe's glanced his way, but no one volunteered to take him home – afraid their cars' interiors might meet the same fate as the sofa's. After cleaning up, Wolfe glanced outside to make certain Guy was still passed out on the ground. He reluctantly called Mr. Butts. He liked the man. He was sorry he had such an idiotic son.

By the time Guy's father's pickup truck pulled alongside his alcohol-sedated form, Guy was rising from the dirt and surveying hazily his surroundings. The disgorging of his stomach made Guy somewhat more lucid, but he was still visibly drunk.

"Oh, hi, Daddy," Guy said heartily. "What brings you out here?"

Mr. Butts's sad eyes glistened displeasure.

"And, Momma, you came along for the ride? A family outing?"

"Get in the truck, Guy," said Lawrence.

"I'm so sorry. I'm so, so sorry," said Guy, stumbling over to the truck and hanging onto Lawrence's open window. "I really messed up badly this time, didn't I?" His eyelids filled with tears, which did not fall. "I'm sorry, Momma and Daddy. Maddie ... everyone just seems so disappointed in me, and I just needed a little drink. Just a little one."

"You're drunk, Guy. Get in the truck!"

Charlene pleaded, "Guy, honey, get in the truck, and we'll take you home. When you didn't show yourself, the reporters left. You just need some rest."

"Okay," said Guy, smiling. "I'll get in the truck on one condition. I'll get in your truck, Daddy, if you let me drive."

"Absolutely not! You get in this truck right now or I'll ..."

"It's been so long since I've driven your truck," whined Guy, opening the driver's side door and pushing on Lawrence's shoulder to move him over."

"You listen to me!" said Lawrence jumping out of the car, grabbing Guy by the shoulders, and shoving his back against the stacked cars.

"Lawrence!" shouted Charlene. "Stop!"

"You are going to get in that … in that truck, and you are going to shut your mouth until we get home, do you hear me?"

"That's from *Hud*, right?" asked Guy, obnoxiously. "Didn't someone in that movie say something like that to his son in *Hud*? Really good, daddy. Great performance."

Lawrence pulled and then pushed Guy back toward the truck, sending him sprawling on the ground.

"Lawrence. Please stop!" shouted Charlene again, exiting the truck.

"You stay there, Charlene. I'm going to get this boy in the truck if it's the last thing I do."

Guy rose, laughing. "All right. All right, Daddy." He swayed to a standing position and then tumbled, still laughing, into the driver's seat. He grabbed the driver's side door, slammed the door shut, and whacked down the lock. He grinned at Lawrence. "Get in, Daddy. I'm going to take us on a family outing. It's been a long time. I'm a good driver … haven't you seen my movie stunts?"

"I'm going to …" said Lawrence, trying to pull up the lock, which had not been used – probably ever – so that it was jammed down inside the door. He grabbed Guy around the collar of his shirt and pulled his head up through the open window. Before Lawrence could say anything more, tears streamed down onto his hand.

"I've been a terrible, terrible son," babbled Guy. "I'm sorry, Daddy. I'm sorry. I just haven't been … things haven't been the best …" He sobbed loudly as Lawrence released his hold.

"Lawrence. Just get in and we'll go. We'll make sure he drives slow. It's not worth all this. Please, Lawrence. *Please*."

Lawrence released his hold on Guy and yielded to his wife's appeal. He slid in next to his wife in the passenger seat.

After a few moments, Guy wiped his face in an attempt at sobriety, shook his head, and said one more "I'm sorry," before he put the pickup in drive and stepped on the gas.

Wolfe was just locking the bar's door when he heard the impact of the truck hitting the tree less than a mile down the dark road.

TWELVE

IT TOOK A FEW DAYS after he awoke for Guy to achieve
a lengthy reclining seated position. Ribs were mostly healed,
though he still took shallow breaths. His leg stayed in a cast for
several more weeks and eventually required another surgery
as well as physical therapy. The puffiness around his broken
face diminished, but his left damaged cheek bone could not
be fully restored. His hair grew back in waves. Thick locks
concealed healed areas on a forehead scarred by broken glass.
His beard emerged in patches, masking some of the havoc
caused by the collision. Evidence of the car accident would be
a lifetime limp and a distorted appearance.

Maddie visited him daily. He was mostly inconsolable since
catching a glimpse of himself in a silver tray on which Annette carried his meds. Leaving, she had tucked it underneath
her arm and turned from him to check his IV. Bewilderingly,
Guy stared at his reflection. His new image was inconceivable.

Guy spoke little to Maddie since his memory exposed that
ugly night. After viewing his reflection, he said nothing. He
simply glowered at her or anyone else who entered the room.

When asked a question, he either remained silent or slowly nodded or shook his head in response.

Though the television in Guy's hospital room was un-plugged – and he never asked for it to be turned on – Maddie caught snippets of the news as she entered and exited other patient rooms. She noted updates on Guy:

"… sustained dramatic facial injuries that have altered his appearance …"

"… likely his future will not include acting …"

"… possibly his last movie … set for release later this summer … likelihood he will not attend opening …"

On a table in the doctors' lounge one day, Maddie noticed a headline in the Charleston paper: "South Carolina's Star Falls."

As his body endeavored to recover, Guy's agent finally arrived in Wynee. Marsha Chambers sported a rented Mercedes from the Charleston International Airport and went directly to the hospital. She was not interested in securing a room at one of the only hospitality centers in Wynee, a new Hampton Inn just off the highway. That is where some of the press had congregated. She hoped not to be there that long. She just wanted to get in, see for herself what the media was reporting, and determine if the end was indeed inevitable for one of her star clients. Guy had refused her telephone calls. And, because of HIPPA laws, she was unable to obtain detailed information about his diagnosis from the hospital over the phone. She had to make the long journey in person just to assess the damage.

Marsha stopped at the hospital gift shop and purchased a bouquet of seasonal flowers in a white vase. Her severely pony-tailed long hair, tailored fuchsia pantsuit with crisp white collared shirt, and sharp, short sentences piqued the curiosity of the shop's manager. When Marsha pulled her credit card from her wallet, the manager studied her face to determine if she was a familiar actress. Smiling awkwardly, the manager finished the transaction.

"Bet a few Lincolns she's come to see our star patient," mumbled the manager to no one after Marsha exited the shop.

Not wanting to alert anyone that she was there, in case Guy refused to see her, she wandered the halls. When a nurse stopped to ask her if she needed help, Marsha inquired as to the location of long-term patients. The nurse eyed her suspiciously and pointed to the opposite end of the hallway.

Marsha walked casually in that direction until she saw a door with a posted "Do Not Disturb" sign. She glanced back down the hallway. No nurses. She turned the door knob and walked boldly inside.

Guy sat upright. A lunch tray had just been delivered and was situated on the movable stand in front of him. It took only a second to register that the woman entering his room was not a nurse.

"Marsha!"

Dismayed, he inadvertently jerked up one knee, flipping the tray of food off the stand and onto the linoleum floor.

He quickly turned his face away from her grimace.

"Please leave!" he said, cowering. "The sign says, 'Do Not Disturb'. Can't you read?!"

"Guy," she began, trying to recover breath that left her when she saw his maimed, unrecognizable face.

"We need to talk."

"About what?" he shouted, curling into the pillow to further hide his face. "What could we possibly have to talk about?"

"You are still under contract for that sequel. We just need to have an understanding … to talk about …" Marsha was finding it difficult to choose the right words.

"Guy, I'm sorry for what you've been through. Truly I am. I'm sorry that you lost your parents. I'm …"

"Get … out!"

"We have a business arrangement, and I need to …"

"Had. *Had* a business arrangement," said Guy, forcefully. "Unless you want to market me as the grotesque and hideous villain … *No makeup necessary!*"

When Marsha did not respond, he continued sarcastically, "No. Didn't think so. Leave! My lawyer can take care of contract matters. You wasted your time coming here. Unless you just wanted to get your own freak peek."

Guy was still twisted toward the wall when Maddie entered; she was followed by the same nurse Marsha met earlier in the hallway.

"What is going on in here?" asked Maddie. "We could hear yelling from the other side of the hospital." She looked at Marsha. "Were you invited into this room?"

"Just leaving," she said, tossing her ponytail off her shoulder and turning toward the door. "I wish you the best, Guy," she said, halfheartedly, exiting between Maddie and the nurse.

Noticing food scattered in every direction on the floor, Maddie turned toward the nurse. "Bring Charlie in to clean this up, please."

When the nurse left, Maddie placed her hand on Guy's arm. He flinched and remained buried in a section of the pillow.

"You okay?"

"Great! Wonderful! Having just a peachy day!"

"I know that was difficult, Guy. But that was just the first of many hurdles," she said, soothingly. "You will have a life again. It just won't be …"

"Oh, so now you're the resident psychiatrist, too?"

"No, Guy, I'm your friend. Or at least I used to be."

"Yeah. You made it pretty clear that night that the friend-ship part was over. I guess we're just down to a physician/patient relationship. And I just don't feel like being psycho-analyzed by a just-out-of-med-school doctor working in a nothing-town hospital."

Stung, she withdrew her hand from his arm.

Guy slackened, his voice still harsh: "You have *no* idea. How could my life possibly be anything after this? How can I move forward? I can't. I will *never* forgive myself for killing my parents … for ruining my career. I have nowhere to go from here. *Nowhere* …"

As Guy spewed remorse, Maddie withered. She desired ur-gently to be away from him. She backed out of his room with-out a word. Blessedly, hospital activity was slow; patients were checked and stable. She informed nurses on duty she was not feeling well and needed rest. She was available by beeper if an emergency arose, she told them. On her way out of the hospital, she saw Stu speaking to a patient. He glanced at her and smiled. She acknowledged him and persisted toward the door.

She had a desperate and inexplicable urge to visit the marsh, where she had not been in years. As she grabbed for the gear shift in her car, she realized her hand was shaking.

She drove from the hospital to the parking lot of Jr.'s Feed and Seed. Mr. Johnson's son had taken over after his father's death from a massive heart attack. Mr. Johnson had packed a handful of fishing worms into a container for a customer, sat down in a chair, and died.

Maddie walked into the store, smiled a hello to Junior Johnson, found the aisle filled floor-to-ceiling with utility boots, pulled a Size 7 Men's off the shelf, and took them to the checkout counter. A Reese's tempted her. She grabbed it and threw it onto the counter as well. She had not eaten breakfast or lunch. *Chocolate and peanut butter soothe the soul*, Miss Sumney liked to say.

Maddie settled back into her car, ate the two gratifying candy disks, and drove to a parking space at the edge of Wynee's downtown. She grabbed the black rubber boots and left her car. She looked around to see if anyone was watching her. Wynee was especially sleepy during weekday mid-afternoons. She marched hastily to the woods that would offer her the path to Newnan's Marsh.

She stopped to pull off clogs and slide bare feet into a dark rubber abyss. After carefully tucking pant legs into the boots, she left the clogs at the side of the path.

The edge of the marsh was less than a quarter mile from the path's entrance. Thankfully, it was low tide. Summer heat on a spring day. She contemplated the marsh's late spring hues, a green palette ranging from pale lime to deep pea to brownish avocado.

Maddie had not traveled to the prairies of the upper mid-West, but she read about them and marveled at the vivid photographs in *National Geographic*. She imagined her marshes resembled the vast plains. A strong breeze – not enough to be called a wind – began at one end, bowing the grass politely in a ripple that stirred a wave of mutable color. In some spots, the grass shimmered a gentle gold.

Maddie paused, considering tragic beauty. A green, captivating sea of emptiness.

She emptied studying it.

She was an orphan twice over; second parents rested side-by-side in Wynee's cemetery, sent there unintentionally by their son's carelessness.

"What's the plan, God?"

She anticipated a response from the limitless marsh.

Waiting, she recalled a passage in one of her favorite childhood books, *Prince Caspian*. Lucy, having not seen Aslan in a while, tells him, "You're bigger."

"That's because you are older, little one," he responds.

"Not because you are?" she asks.

"I am not. But every year you grow you will find me bigger."

As a child, she pondered relentlessly the last line to understand the riddle.

Gazing at the marsh, she felt minute. He was big. It was *all* too big. How could she possibly help Guy without losing herself?

She waded into the marsh, gingerly at first. Her feet sunk with each step, making a dreadful sucking sound. The pluff-mud struggled against her, grasping her boots. Indignation discharged with each exertion, with each menacing noise of rubber releasing from a muddy hold. Determination moved her forward; she spoke a word – quietly at first – then with intensifying vigor the farther she ventured.

"Why … did … you … do … this?!"

"WHAT … DO … YOU … WANT … ME … TO … DO … *NOW*?!"

Tears spilled onto cheeks flushed with anger and exhaustion. Her shirt soaked through from perspiration. She stopped and picked up two handfuls of the dark goo beneath her. She threw them forcefully into the air.

"*I don't understand!*" she screamed.

"I don't understand!" Maddie wailed over and over again until the words became a whisper, and then a prayer.

"Lord, I don't understand what you want me to do here. I can't figure this out on my own. Help me. Please."

Maddie stooped, defeated, several yards from the shoreline, in the marsh. Her hands to her wrists were dark brown from the pluffmud.

Tell him.

It entered her mind clearly; almost audibly.

Tell him.

Tell him.

Maddie wiped her eyes with the back of her forearm. She stood for several moments, her eyes fixed on the immeasurable space before her.

She turned, relieved, and headed back toward the shore.

THIRTEEN

AFTER THE UNANNOUNCED VISIT BY HIS AGENT, Guy spent another week in the Wynee General Hospital before he was in any shape to be released. A plastic surgeon had been called up from Charleston to determine if more could be done to reduce the scarring that demarcated his face. Guy immediately dismissed the surgeon, growling at him: "If I want more work done on this face, it won't be by some lowcountry doctor."

The nurses and staff at Wynee General were more than anxious to discharge him – as was Maddie. He fumed at her whenever she entered the room. He no longer sought her with a child-like, yearning for consolation. Guy saw her as a stinging reminder of his parents, of that night. Maddie's presence intensified the potency of hopelessness. In her white coat, security tag hanging about her neck, her future glared secure. His was obliterated.

Maddie tried repeatedly to speak to him, to offer him encouragement. Guy bristled, interpreting her approach as condescending. Light that had eked in on their shelved relationship directly after the accident dimmed. Maddie believed she could not and would not be able to reach him.

"Whooeee," expressed Annette as she entered the nurse's station to update files. "He's a tough one. Won't be none too sorry to see him go. Think he lost all sense of manners out there in ol' Follywood."

"Amen to that," said Dr. Ledger, giving Annette a pat on the back. "I don't think anyone will be sorry to see him go." Maddie poured over her charts, ignoring the banter.

"Ya know. I feel sorry for him," said Annette. "He's as rude and arrogant as hell, but I think he felt safe here. He's on his own out there."

"His choice," said Stu. He glanced over at Maddie, who seemed to be engrossed in her charts. A recent private conversation over dinner a week earlier imbued him to speak unreservedly about the dynamics of Maddie and Guy's relationship. She shared with Stu her feelings towards Guy, their connected past, and the frustrations she felt about not knowing how to proceed. She did not tell him everything, but she let him enter in a bit further.

"He's like family to me," explained Maddie. "The only semblance of family I have left. I feel some obligation to him."

"Are you sure that's it?" he had asked her.

"What do you mean?"

"I mean, Maddie, I care about you, and I feel like we're progressing. Your feelings for Guy seem fairly deep, and I just want to know, honestly, that you're not anticipating something more from him that's beyond friendship."

"No, Stu. I may have toyed around with it in the past, but I really don't think we were meant for that path. I just … well, I feel bonded to him in a way that's … different. I don't know. God knit us together … our lives … but not in the way that He knits people together for a marriage. It's hard to explain.

I'm just trying to figure out if there is anything else I can do to help him."

"You've helped fix him physically. That's your job. You can't fix him emotionally and mentally. It's going to take a power greater than yourself to take on that task."

Stu – wise, patient, steady. Some solace for the turmoil she felt within.

Guy left the hospital and settled into the only place he knew and could hide: his parents' home. After lingering engrossingly at his reflection in the powder room mirror near the entryway only minutes after he first entered the home, he ripped it from the wall – leaving the fittings exposed. He deposited it into the large trash container at the back of the house. He did the same with the other mirrors. One by one. He searched out table mirrors and even his mother's antique, gilded vanity mirror. Eliminated.

He drew closed heavy brocade draperies. Darkness crept in corners.

While Guy convalesced in the hospital, neighbors had taken turns maintaining the Butts's yard and the flower beds. When Guy established himself in the home, they stopped. Word of his venomous demeanor in the hospital spread as if ants shared information in a colony. Dismayed Wyneeans shook their heads. *What a waste*, they whispered on porches and in the food aisles. Some prayed. Collectively, they agreed there was no need to keep up the grounds at the house; surely he would hire someone to maintain it. He did not. The weeds grew high around the massive white structure. They choked out the flowers. Strangely, the bottles and wind chimes hanging in the trees gradually disappeared. Wyneeans never really approved anyway. With the general dishevelment of the place, no one seemed to notice they were gone.

A few heart-heavy residents, those who had been especially close to Lawrence and Charlene, left cakes, biscuits, and fresh picked produce on the screened-in back porch – for a short time. They knocked, but no response. They telephoned; no answer. When Fran called Barbara Ellen to tell her that the food she left early in the week was still sitting there, thus ended Wyneean charity. It could only go so far.

For the first few weeks, Maddie stopped by daily. She entered the house without invitation. Initially, she found Guy lying on his childhood bed in his old upstairs room staring at the God's eye. She checked to make certain he had not taken too much pain medication, then she would ask him the same questions:

"Have you eaten today?"

"Some."

"Are you in pain?"

"Some."

"Have you done the exercises for your leg that the physical therapist prescribed?

"Yeah."

"Can I get you anything?"

"No."

Maddie tried to force herself to confront him – to wrangle him from his resignation. She remembered her time in the marsh. She was not ready; she did not feel bold enough or strong enough. She could not put her finger on why. She yielded to an inner tug to check on him daily, but she did not want to be there. She prickled from head to toe with unease. She wanted to shriek at him:

You brought this on yourself! Deal with it!

She kept silent. She accepted his deep remorse and self-loathing and it stirred compassion in her. She allowed him to wallow. She prayed to find the right time, or let that right time find her.

That right time was on the day she discovered the doors to the Butts's house locked. Unyielding, she stood at the back door contemplating a next move.

"Guy! Open this door!"

She waited. No answer.

"Guy … seriously! Open the door!" She rattled the handle and waited. *Jerk*, she muttered, exasperated.

She could smash a pane in the back door, reach her hand in, and unlock it. She would explain to Guy that she thought the worst, which she was actually thinking. Her heart raced. She picked up a loose brick from the back stoop. She lifted her arm high with the brick in her hand.

"Madeline Louise Walker!"

Maddie whirled around to see Squash, hands on her hips, standing in the yard.

"Lord, child. You as crazy as he is?"

Maddie lowered the brick.

"He's not answering!"

"I know he's not answerin', It's becausa' me, probably. That boy's bad off, but I don't think he's *that* bad off. Not to do somethin' to himself. He's just blistered 'cause a what I said to him yesterday, and he's tryin' to shut us all out. I just had it yesterday when I walked by here. His momma's gardens are all gone. The weeds is takin' over everything. The yard's more of an embarrassment to the memory of those God-fearin' folks now that they're gone than it was when they were alive. It's disgraceful," she paused, visibly riled. She swept her hand around while she talked, surveying the disheveled condition of the yard. "I just marched right in there and told him that he's hirin' me to clean up this place, inside and out. I've got Mr. Harry from down my way bringin' his ridin' lawn mower. A few of my neighbor boys who ain't doin' nothin' this summer but lazyin' around and tryin' to think of someway to get into trouble are comin' to help me pull them weeds. I told that no good boy up there," she lifted her eyes to the second story window, "that we're not lettin' this house fall to the worms."

She went on, "He don't like it none. Told me to get the you-know-what blankety, blank, I ain't repeatin' it, h-e-l-l out of his house. He's in the pit right now Maddie. Wallerin' in it. Good and deep, that pit is. Stuck up in that mire like he ain't never gonna get out. But you just keep visitin' him, and he'll come around."

"But what if …"

"His story's not over yet, child," she said, sensing Maddie's concerns. "It's just a chapter. A bad, bad chapter. Yes. But a chapter. That's all. He'll have some good chapters after this. He might just need you to help him know his story better. Fill in the blanks. He doesn't really know what's happened here. There's miracles in tragedies, child. Yes, miracles in tragedies. Show him the good. There's always some light in the dark."

Maddie stared at her, dumbfounded. *Tell him*, resonated in her mind. Squash grabbed the brick out of Maddie's limp hand. Instead of smashing the whole window pane as Maddie had intended to do, she expertly tapped one corner in a semi-circle until the glass cracked and a piece fell, leaving a space just large enough for Squash to fit her small hand into. As Maddie eyed her warily, Squash carefully protruded her hand through the opening, feeling for the lock on the door handle. Turning it, she pulled her hand out and opened the back door of the house. Squash smiled smugly at Maddie and winked an eye.

"Done this before a time or two?" asked Maddie.

"Don't you salt me none girl," Squash winked again. "I can still put a whoopin' on you!"

Maddie shook her head; a smile attempted to work its way onto her strained expression.

"Have at him," said Squash, turning from the door.

"Where are you going?"

"Lord, child, I've got days and days of work in this yard to do. I've gotta get to it."

The kitchen was the only room bathed in light. It had no curtains or blinds to block out the sun's rays. Maddie noticed instantly that a dirty plate and cup lay in the sink, while an empty can of Campbell's tomato soup and a pack of half-eaten crackers littered the counter. She washed the two dishes, dried them, put them away. She threw away the can and crackers, wiped up the tiny trail of sugar ants invading the abandoned food, and took a deep breath. She stood in the kitchen, staring blankly at the kitchen cabinets, wondering why. Why had a friendship solidified so long ago? As Squash alluded to once, only God could have orchestrated such a union. Despite the present circumstances, their friendship rooted her life. With Guy she had the sweetness and thrill of an exceptional childhood. His parents had poured the foundation for her faith. Of all the families in Wynee, God chose the one carrying shame to be the improbable blessing in a lonely, motherless, workaholic doctor's daughter's life. Through this, a healing salve gradually covered the wound. She was brought to this moment. It all made sense to her how the friendship had fortified forgiveness for past transgressions, and it was necessary now to open Guy's eyes to that forgiveness.

Maddie departed the security of the lighted kitchen and entered the inky interior of the vast home. As she ambled tentatively through the house, she paused to pull back the impermeable velvet drapes and twist the arm on the plantation blinds. She shielded her eyes from the blinding light that instantly illuminated hibernating corners.

She glided quietly through the formal dining room, the living room, and into the great hallway. She listened at the bottom of the stairs but heard nothing. She walked slowly up the wide stairway, steadying herself on the rosewood banister. She mustered determination with each step. But when she came to his room, the door was open, and Guy was not inside.

She felt a panic clutch her. She searched the other upstairs rooms, and the bathrooms. All the doors were open – no Guy. She hurried back down the stairs. *The library.*

Maddie made her way through the parlor and into another, smaller hallway to the closed door of the library. A thin light peered from beneath the door.

Timidly, lightly, she knocked.

"Guy."

She heard shuffling. She released a breath she did not realize she was holding.

"Guy."

She turned the door knob and entered the dank room. It smelled of musty books. Guy sat at his father's antique walnut desk with tooled leather top. Books and papers spread to both ends. Guy looked up at her from his father's leather button-tufted desk chair. It was the first time she had seen him sitting upright in days. His lengthening hair stuck out in places from neglect; his beard equally mussed. Healing pinkish scars contrasted with a pasty complexion. His expression: stone.

Her eyes lowered onto a small revolver decorated with white mother-of-pearl. It waited beside his right hand.

Hoarsely he uttered, "Who's Greta?"

She felt her throat tighten, obstructing words she knew needed to form swiftly.

"Greta! I … asked … you … a question! Who is Greta? Did you happen to know anyone named Greta, Maddie?"

An enormous, well-worn Bible resided, open, on his father's desk. With a fixed, cold mien, Guy pointed to a page, poking it harshly.

"It says here, right here in Ezekiel, 'Rid yourself of all the offenses you have committed and get a new heart and a new spirit.' It says right here in the margin, 'I'm sorry, Greta.' Who the fu …"

"Guy."

He lifted his head from the page, glowering at her. Maddie's eyes pleaded with him to stop.

Guy looked down at the Bible again, flipping wildly through the pages. "I found her name on some other pages, too. 'I'm sorry, Greta,' right next to all the Psalms David wrote after Bathsheba. 'I'm sorry, Greta.' Here," he hammered the book with his finger and turned the pages. "'I'm sorry, Greta!' Here again. Who's Greta, Maddie!? Tell me, dammit!"

Guy stood up and pounded his fist on the open page of the Bible. Maddie winced. She worked harder to find her voice.

"*Greta … Greta … Greta*! Not a real common everyday name here in the good ol' South, is it, Maddie?!" he thundered. "It was your *mother's* name though, wasn't it, Maddie?! Not Caroline or Anna Katherine or Elizabeth Jane like every second person in this God-forsaken dot-on-the-map. But *Gre-ta*! Why … is … *your* … mother's … name … in … *my* … father's … Bible?!"

He paused, eyeing her piercingly.

Maddie thought of turning and walking – *running* – away from his hostility. She fought against cowardice and stationed herself. *Tell him*.

"Guy," she eased, steadily. "There are many things I would like to talk to you about … to tell you. But I won't talk to you while you are in this state. Take a shower. Shave. I'll take you to visit your parents' grave. Everyone's at work right now. No one will bother us. We'll talk."

Downcast, as if scolded for muddy footprints on a white carpet, Guy gazed vacantly and then lowered dejectedly back into the leather chair. He glanced at the gun. He dropped his head into his hands; fingertips gripped at his furrowed brow. The silence climbed flights of stairs until Maddie could bear it no longer. She turned to leave.

Guy heard the wooden floor board screak with her intended departure. "Please don't," he muttered. He lifted his face and walked, trance-like, from behind the desk. He wore his father's bathrobe. His feet were bare. "I'll clean up and we can go."

Sluggishly, he left the room.

As soon as Maddie heard the shower water running, she grabbed the gun. She searched the drawers of the desk and every dark crevice of the built-in book shelves for the existence of another weapon. She checked inside drawers and under the beds of his bedroom and his parents' room. The pantry and china cabinets were investigated. Satisfied no other guns existed, she quickly descended the stairs, ran into the backyard, and directly into Squash pushing a wheelbarrow – soiled green garden gloves on her hands.

"Mary and Joseph! Child, what are you doing? Give me that gun!"

"Hide it, Squash. Dig a deep hole while you're weeding and hide it in there. He had it sitting on Lawrence's desk when I walked it."

"I knowed he was bad off, but he's a right bit worse than I expected."

"Well, he's agreed to go with me to visit his parents' grave. I'm going to tell him then," said Maddie.

"Tell him what?" asked Squash.

"That goodness can come out of forgiveness."

"I expects it's about time he knows that. Expects it's about time." She took the gun from Maddie's hand, made sure the safety was secure, and stuck it into her pocket. Then she grabbed for the same hand that a second ago held the instrument that could have easily ended Guy's life. Squash maternally caressed Maddie's hand before she spoke.

"I'm praying for you, child. Right now and all day long 'cause you're going to need it. But let me tell you something. You're exactly where you needs to be right here at this moment in you two's lives, and you'll know exactly the right words to spill out of your mouth at the right time that you need to be spillin' 'em. That's my prayer."

"Thank you, Squash." Maddie leaned over and kissed her on the check, a rare gesture that brought a buoyant look to the dark woman's face.

Maddie watched from the back porch as Squash first placed the gun on the ground as if it were a diseased, dead squirrel, and then deluged it with the watering hose. She used a shovel to scoop it up and carry it to a tangled area under a pine tree. She dug a deep, narrow hole before gingerly dropping it in, covering it, brushing the area over with pine straw and debris, and readjusting a thorny bush serving as sentry.

"Goin' to keep that little area natural," she said, winking. "Ain't goin' to be yankin' on no weeds or dressin' it … can just stay wild and crazy and don't nobody have to know why. We'll tell people that's how Charlene woulda' wanted it and they won't think twice 'bout it." She winked again at Maddie and set off for another area of the yard.

Maddie went into the kitchen and prepared a sandwich for Guy; she was glad to have a menial task to douse her apprehension while she waited for him to emerge.

Guy eventually hobbled, clean shaven, into the kitchen. He wore an old USC baseball cap low on his forehead, a navy t-shirt, and loose-fitting khaki pants. Humidity and heat of dog days lingered, yet Guy's badly scarred legs hid within cotton fabric. Shorts were not a consideration; shame overruled comfort.

"It looks like you ate something earlier, but I made you a sandwich in case …"

"That was yesterday," he said, darkly. He sat down at the table and waited for Maddie to bring the sandwich. He ate it, slowly, looking only at his plate.

Unsure of her next move, she stood patiently at the sink.

Guy finished his sandwich, downed a glass of iced tea, and urged himself up from the chair. He walked carefully out the kitchen door. Maddie heard a car door open and close. When she looked out the kitchen window, Guy sat in the passenger seat of her car, his gaunt, mending face staring straight ahead.

As a last minute thought, Maddie went through the house to the front door. Beside it was an umbrella stand with two antique canes that Lawrence had admired and purchased some years before. She grabbed the one with the bronze eagle's head.

"What's that for?" asked Guy, eyeing the cane as she slipped it into the back seat of her car.

"It's a long walk from the entrance of the cemetery to your parents' grave. You might need it."

"Hmmft!" he said, a scowl consuming his face.
Maddie ignored him. They drove the two miles to Wynee Cemetery in expected silence.

Flanking an ornate aged wrought iron gate were two massive oaks; on every low sprawling branch lounged a dense cluster of Spanish moss – expressing death, though seething with inaudible life.

Maddie pulled onto a gravel patch near the entrance, grabbed the eagle-headed cane, and walked around to Guy's side. She waited as he concentrated on maneuvering his debilitated legs. He managed himself out of the car. She offered him the cane, but he refused. She carried it, just in case.

In silence, they crept along the crumbling brick path; Guy steadied himself against a tree or a bush each time he faltered over an uneven area. As they made their way through the ancient enclosure, they passed common names of the area: Lipscomb, Wilson, Anderson, DuBoise. Some white marble markers were neatly kept, while others wore their neglect. Droppings of Spanish moss obscured the path or draped indiscriminately on grave stones.

Guy paused on the grayish green path and grabbed the cane from Maddie. Fatigue edged his face. He proceeded without a word, the tip of the cane clicking drearily on the worn bricks.

They came to an area of freshly turned earth. An elder at the Baptist church, who passed peacefully in his sleep at 92, was interred there two days previously. Only a few feet beyond the still-fresh gravesite were tombstones for Lawrence and Charlene Butts.

"The boundary lines have fallen for me in pleasant places; surely I have a delightful inheritance." The words were inscribed below each of their names, along with *Wife and Mother* under her name and *Husband and Father* under his.

Guy leaned heavily on the cane, grasping firmly the bird's head. He stared at the erect granite slabs for some minutes. "Who decided on *those* words for the inscription?" He pointed at the headstones with the end of the cane. Revulsion beleaguered his already damaged features.

"According to Fred Larkin, the attorney, the will was in the top drawer of your daddy's desk in the magistrate office," said Maddie. "He had it all spelled out … his wishes, and the wishes of your mother. Remember, I told you Mr. Larkin still needs to go over the will with you. You said you weren't ready. He said he wants me to be there, too, that I'm mentioned in it."

"What's that from?" asked Guy, pointing at the verse on the headstones.

"The Bible."

"*I know that*," he scowled. "What book?"

"It's from Psalm 16," she responded, unfazed. She was determined to get through intact and unshaken by his piteous demeanor.

He glared again at the gravestones. Fury loitered on his features, but Maddie noticed his eyes heavy with unshed tears.

"So, you wanted to talk," he said, breaking the stoic spell. Guy faltered to a wrought iron garden bench and leaned himself against its back. Facing it was a marble seat decorated at the base with faceless angels. Maddie seated herself there and leaned in toward him, her elbows resting on her knees, her hands folded, as if in prayer.

She drew in a breath, ready to deliver the dialogue repeated over and over again in the car on the drive to his house and in the kitchen as she waited for Guy to finish showering.

"Did your mother have an affair with my father?" he blurted.

Shocked, Maddie faltered. "Yes … no … well, sort of … I …"

"Damn! Damn it, Maddie!" said Guy, banging the eagle's head on the arm of the bench. "Did you know about this when we were kids? No wonder your father didn't want us playing together … no wonder Squash …" He struck the bench again with the head of the cane and shook his head.

"Guy! Let me explain to you what happened."

Trembling, he scanned the cemetery. He growled low: "*Nothing* makes sense to me anymore, Maddie."

Tears, long bolted, emptied over his lower lids. He crumpled forward. Maddie moved to his side, engaging her hand with his back. Guy wept convulsively, his spine heaving up and down under her palm.

For several moments, Maddie steadied beside him. She waited. His soulful cry moved in her a mother's compassion. Tenderly, her hand drifted to the back of his head and stroked his hair. She pulled him closer, consenting to a cascade of pent-up remorse.

When his lament ended, he wiped his face with the t-shirt hem and lifted his head. Maddie simultaneously released her motherly grasp. Weakened from the deluge, Guy's tone abated.

"Tell me what happened with our parents, Maddie, before all this … before …" he said, raspy, glancing in the direction of their gravesite, "before I killed them."

Maddie took his hand. He allowed her to hold it, gently. As Maddie's words discharged, Guy fixed his gaze on the mossy path in front of him and listened.

"Squash offered it all to me after Daddy died. Actually, I asked her outright when she was there with me going through his things. There were pictures of Momma and Daddy together before I was born. They seemed happy enough, but I never could get Daddy to tell me any stories about her. His face would get all clouded up and angry looking when I mentioned her. Sort of angry-sad. So I just confronted Squash. I told her, 'I know something happened to make my Momma fall down our stairs. I know it had to do with Mr. Butts. Now I want you to tell me what happened.' So she did. You know how Squash seems to just know everything about everyone … all the details. Well, she knew about this. Your daddy and my

Momma worked together at the school. Then Momma got pregnant with me and was supposedly really sick ..."

"Oh God, Maddie ... No ... *No* ... I can't, never mind ... I ..."

"We're not ... siblings, Guy. I know. That's what I was worried about too. No. In fact, it all started out innocent enough, according to Squash. He found her in the school's parking lot throwing up. He helped her into the building, put a wet cloth on her head, and nursed her. She would have to leave meetings because she was sick, and stay in the bathroom for a long time. My daddy worked all the time, so Momma probably wasn't getting any attention from him. Your daddy gave her some attention when she needed it. They just got more and more comfortable with one another, Squash told me, and I think your daddy must have fallen in love with her."

Guy continued studying the greenish growth on the walkway, seemingly unmoved.

"Well, who knows what all happened between them. She *was* pregnant. I can't imagine there was too much of a romance. Then your own mother got pregnant. Instead of acting happy about it, your daddy didn't even tell anyone he worked with at the school about it. Charlene just began to show and that's how people found out. That's how Momma found out. People saw her crying at work ... saw your daddy short-tempered. Evidently, there was one scene in the parking lot when she was leaving to go home. He grabbed her arm and was pleading with her.

"Squash said she just heard from people that the tension was there between them, with your daddy acting erratic and Momma crying a lot – not too sure how either of them wanted it to all to play out. Then Momma had me, and Squash said there were a few months there at the beginning – when Momma was on her maternity leave from the school – that she seemed settled. She and Daddy seemed okay together. Squash said they showed me around town. What happened at the school seemed to go away. As far as Squash knew, neither Daddy nor Charlene suspected anything at this point.

"But then your daddy showed up at my house one night." Guy stiffened and drew his hand away from Maddie's.

"Do you want me to go on?" asked Maddie.

"Of course," he murmured.

"Squash said she was at the house that night because my daddy had already hired her to help out. Squash was in the pantry organizing a space for the baby food and bottles. She said Momma wasn't the best at organizing. She said Daddy was home, in his study reading the paper with me asleep on his lap. But his car wasn't in the driveway because it sputtered and died at the hospital, and he just walked home that night. Lawrence must have thought he wasn't home because he just came right in the back door and called out to Momma. He seemed to be in a frenzy; that's the way Squash described him. He just walked right in and called, 'Greta!' really loudly. He didn't see Squash. Didn't stop to pay attention to anything. Momma was upstairs and she ran to the top of the stairs and waved her hands and put her finger to her mouth for him to be quiet. He was on a mission, Squash said. Your father was pleading, half crying, telling her he was sorry – to please forgive him for all of it. Squash said Momma was just holding up her hands for him to be quiet and taking one step at a time, looking over the banister to see if my father heard him.

"My father did hear. He came out of his study holding me in his arms, and he looked up at Momma on the stairs and at Lawrence and asked, 'What's happening here?' Squash said Momma just let out a cry and her foot slipped on the next step and she came tumbling down. Daddy yelled for Squash to come and he handed me to her. Then he checked Momma and called for an ambulance. Squash said he just kept repeating, 'No, No, No,' over and over again. She said she didn't know what happened to Lawrence. He was there and then he wasn't."

Guy lifted his gaze from the path in front of him. He turned and stared vacantly at Maddie. He stabbed the cane into the ground and rose, steadying both hands on the eagle's head. He looked down at her. He sniffed and shook his head incredulously. He scanned the cemetery once more before his discourse: "*Why* did you think this was a good idea? To tell me this, *now*? Did you think that this would make me feel *better*?! Or are you *purposely* trying to load more guilt on me?"

"Guy, let me …"

"I already know that the only thing left of my parents – because of *me*, mind you – is that rock over there with their names and some corny religious message, and now you're telling me that you grew up without a mother because of my father!"

As his voice elevated, he twisted the point of the cane into the dirt hollowing a small crater. "Unbelievable." He shook his head and laughed mockingly. "Purely unbelievable. This is like one of those dark, tragic movies my father sometimes watched, except I'm right smack in the middle of it! Ha! This time the great producer Himself made it so that I get to play the crippled freak for the rest of my life. Serves me right, though, huh!"

"But, Guy, don't you see the miracle in all this?" She moved toward him and thought better of it.

"The miracle? *The miracle?* That's a good one, Maddie," he said, grimacing. "Ha! Ha! A miracle! I guess it's a miracle I'm not buried six feet under rotting with them!"

"No, Guy. It's a miracle that all was forgiven … that we came together as friends. Our friendship brought about healing, and it made a way for your father to make amends for what happened. He doted on me like I was his own daughter, and your mother did as well. And they stayed together through it all; that's a miracle in itself. And when my father was dying, he looked at me and smiled and said, 'It's okay, butterfly.' He had to have known I was sneaking around with you all that time when we were younger. He had to have known how important my friendship with you and your parents was. Yet, in his way, he had forgiven your father. I'm sure of it. It was a tragic thing that happened. But Guy, you have no idea how your family blessed my childhood. There's good that's come from this. There is."

Tears sealed determinedly broke free. She stood and grabbed his arm. "Guy, please." His angry demeanor steeled. He withdrew from her gesture.

"Take me home," he said, hobbling in the direction of the car.

Maddie stood alone on the path, allowing the tears to flow.

No more words passed between them in the car. In silence, she slowed in front of grand fluted columns guarding a white entryway before easing down the gravel drive leading to the back of the home. Maddie opened her door in order to help Guy, but he held up a hand to stop her. "No," he said emphatically.

"I won't be coming back here," said Maddie, spent. "If you want to speak to me or need me for something, you know where I am."

Guy walked resolutely toward the back door. He did not acknowledge Maddie as she left him.

FOURTEEN

TWO WEEKS LATER, Maddie was sitting in the law office of attorney Fred Larkin on Waterside Street. His office, in a 19th century two-story brick building, overlooked a small dock where local fishermen tied their buckboards. Fred lived upstairs. He never married and the law office was passed down to him by his father, who was a lawyer prominent not only in tiny Wynee – but known to take thorny cases in Charleston or even in the Upstate. Fred, though, kept close to home. He was a subdued version of his father, whose legal engines revved at the thought of a criminal trial. Fred preferred wills, deeds, and contracts. An occasional departure was negotiating a settlement in a civil dispute; yet those churned him at night. He preferred no-frills, no-mess lawyering.

Each morning, after lingering over coffee and the *Charleston Post and Courier*, he meandered down creaky steps to a monotonous office with the same dowdy oak furniture his father used. The only technological advancements to the space were a plug-in calculator and a digital clock. Lurlene did his billing by hand and kept his files. They were a long-time couple, just not the marrying kind. On occasion, she tried convincing her beau that a computer was not such a bad idea. "There's lots of things that people said weren't such a bad idea that ended up being really bad ideas," he told her. End of subject – until she brought it up again.

Larkin did not own a car. If he wanted to go somewhere, he walked, rain or shine, in his good suit, from his office to Main. There he tended to bank matters. He sat in the same booth at Lola Ann's Cafeteria for breakfast and lunch, and he picked up what he needed for his home at Chip's General Store and Funeral Home. Often he visited with clients while at Chip's.

Fred Larkin was too tight for pretention; unadorned, passive even, but he was steady and trustworthy and anyone who was someone in Wynee went to him for their wills.

Maddie liked Fred – had looked in on him earlier in the year after he was treated for a blocked carotid artery. She sat upright and uncomfortable in the slatted-back oak chair; she watched him open an antique safe and pull out the will of Lawrence Butts.

"He said he would be here," muttered Larkin, closing the safe. "How's he been doing?" he turned to face Maddie.

"I haven't spoken to him in a few weeks," she answered.

"Still holed up in that house then, huh?"

"I suppose." Maddie was quiet for a moment and then said, "Frankly, Mr. Larkin, I would prefer just to do this alone. Does Guy really need to be here?"

"Yes. It was at his father's request that at least the portion of the will that pertains to you be read with both of you present. Is there a problem?"

"It's just very difficult to …"

Before she could explain, Guy entered the office. Maddie gasped, and then tried to cover it with a cough. She glanced at Mr. Larkin, whose face responded to the piteous sight before him. He stuck out his hand and forced a "hello" toward Guy, but his expression was one of aversion.

Guy's gaunt face was splotched with crimson. His beard, a snarled and overgrown mass, publicized his state of mind. He leaned on a cane in the doorway, but hastily propped it in the entryway corner and shuffled achingly to the only other chair in Larkin's meager office. It was not until Guy sat down that he strained a "hello," but did not make eye contact with Maddie.

"Well, I know that neither of you came here to chitchat with me," said Fred, after a bothersome moment of dead air. "Let's just get on with this." He turned to Guy. "When your father came to me concerning his will about three years ago, he made the unusual request that Maddie be present. I told him this was out of the ordinary, but he explained that it was simply his wish. First, I'll read the part of his will that pertains to her, and then we can go over the rest of it."

He began reading. Maddie was to inherit from him a few antiques from their home, namely the German grandfather clock in their dining room that she had admired since first gracing their table as a child.

Maddie, nervous but static, listened while he read the legalese, her hands folded in her lap. From her vantage point, she observed Guy's demeanor. His miserable appearance compressed her heart. Part of her was tempted to interrupt the meeting and do *something* to break the spell of woeful-ness that hung on Guy like a burdensome woolen coat. Yet, that garment, by all visible accounts, was made of hardened concrete impregnable to any outpouring of human empathy. His contempt for himself and for everyone around him, her included, would define him now. Her attempts to reach him had been and would be fruitless. Out of respect, she would listen to why Lawrence wanted her there, and then she would try to close the door. Let him sit under his tamarisk tree.

After the attorney told her of the items she was to inherit from the house, he handed her an envelope. She looked at it curiously and then her eyes returned to Fred's face. Maddie held the sealed envelope carefully in the open palm of her right hand. She held it, stared down at it, and then back up at the attorney.

"What's this?"

"He wants you to read it."

"So I'm done?"

"He wants you to read it *out loud* ... here."

"I can't take this home and read it?" she asked, incredulously.

"He requested that you read it here. He was probably concerned that you might not ever open that envelope. It's my job as his attorney to push through with his wishes. Please open the envelope and read it while you're in my presence."

She stole a glance at Guy. Impassive, he stared blankly in her direction. She looked back down at the outwardly innocuous envelope, wishing its disappearance, dreading its contents. She pulled her breath in slowly and then, upon exhaling, tore the seal. She unfolded the white paper. Lawrence's hand filled pages from top to bottom. She began:

> *Dearest Maddie,*
>
> *If you are reading this, I am gone and Charlene is gone, as I have asked Mr. Larkin to present this letter to you after we have both passed. I hope as I write this letter that our exits are to be peaceful ones, but somewhere down deep in my soul, I suspect that they will not be. I've been persuaded by Him many times to write you this letter, which makes me think it is needed for whatever reason. He knows. That is*

all that matters. If I had been a braver man, I would have spoken these words to you in person. But I did not, because I am not.

By now I can only imagine you know what happened to your mother and why. This is such a small town, and Ms. Sumney was present when it happened. I would suppose she has spoken to you. There was a time when you returned to Wynee after college that I sensed you knew. I am not sure why. I just had a feeling about it. I prayed that you did know, for then it meant that you had somehow forgiven me without me asking for it.

I often ask Him, 'What were you thinking?' I can't imagine, except that knowing you made our lives richer – and Guy's life fuller and more meaningful. I would not have come to faith if not for this tragedy, and I would not have had the opportunity to help lead you there. So, without truly trying to understand His ways, because they are not our ways, all that I can interpret is that with your mother's loss, some souls were gained.

But if you do not know, this letter is confusing you. Let me begin by telling you that I fell in love with your mother when she was pregnant with you. She was so, so sick every day at Riley Halls where we worked together. An unlikely romance, yes, but it happened. I suppose I felt like the knight in her distress, and it overtook me so that I did not use discretion. I loved Charlene immensely and it had nothing to do with my love for her. It is difficult to explain, but I felt an overwhelming protective love over your mother, Greta, that I had never experienced before. Let me tell you now, before you wad up this letter and destroy it, that there was nothing overtly physical to this encounter (I hesitate to label it a relationship). It was more emotionally intimate than physically intimate. Your mother accepted my attention and concern, *and I know she had feelings for me too, but when I finally revealed the depth of my feelings for her, tried to kiss her, begged her – in my moment of weakness – to go anywhere away with me, she told me she could not and would not.*

After she took maternity leave and had you, I felt such awful remorse. I horribly regretted allowing such feelings to overtake me. I confessed what I had done to Charlene and asked her for forgiveness; I pleaded with her to let me make things right between us. She consented. But I felt strongly that I also needed to apologize to your mother – for causing such an emotional upheaval in our lives. On impulse, I left my office on an early evening a few months after you were born and walked by the hospital to make certain your father's car was still parked there. Then I walked straight to your house. I just wanted to apologize in person, and that would be the end of it. Oh, Maddie. It was the wrong, wrong, wrong thing for me to do. When I saw her expression as she stood at the top of the stairs, I immediately knew she thought I was there to beg some more. I tried to tell her why I was there as she stepped onto the stairs, but it all happened so fast. She was so flustered because   as I quickly learned – your father was home. Maddie. Oh, Maddie. My heart breaks again to tell you this. I am completely responsible for your mother's death. Completely. My selfishness … foolishness, killed her. And I am so, so sorry Maddie.

I tell you the truth when I tell you this, it was only by God's grace that I was able to function after that night. I was a coward; I fled from your home instead of stay and face your father. I had no idea if she was alright. I was devastated to learn she had died from the fall. I wanted him to come and kill me. I wanted to kill myself, but I was a coward even in that.

*But Maddie, it was this tragedy, Guy's birth, and
Charlene's needs that pushed me toward Him ... brought
me finally to my knees, literally. I'm so sorry, Maddie, and I
needed you to know that. Even though I never felt that I had
a right to, I loved you as I would have loved a daughter. I
have made huge mistakes in my life, but there is one mistake
I do not regret making, and that is allowing you and Guy
to be friends. It went against everything inside me when you
showed up in our yard that day. I would have moved away
from Wynee after your mother's death and never returned if
it had not been for Charlene's insistence that we stay. I didn't
even want to look at you, for I felt such guilt, much less have
you as a constant reminder of what I did. But God spoke so,
so clearly to me one day: "You have assigned me my portion
and my cup ..." What I had learned shortly thereafter is
that He gave Charlene those same exact words from Psalm
16. That was our conviction, and after we prayed about
it together – because by that time the hurt between us had
knitted us so closely together – we decided that the friendship
was to be a mighty blessing. And it has been – for all of us.*

*I know that Guy has left us – at least at the writing of
this letter we have heard from him, but not spent time with
him in several years. We don't blame him. We pushed him
toward it. Our crazy interest in movies. What else would he
have become, but an actor!*

*However, there may come a time when he will return
and may need your friendship more than he realizes. He may
need you now, especially that we are gone. Be there for him.
That is my dying wish. That you would forgive all, and
that you would be there for our son.*

Love to you across the heavenly realm – Lawrence

Maddie choked on the last few lines, yet did not yield to
sentiment. She grasped the letter, not wanting to look up from

it. She was aware of a tear working its way onto her eyelid, of a sob building in her diaphragm. She managed to stand and forced a formal "thank you" toward Fred. She turned to Guy and dropped the letter into his lap. She squeezed his shoulder and permitted her hand to linger there – for a moment. *Deep calls to deep.* Then she walked out of the office and closed the door.

FIFTEEN

MADDIE was spooning strawberries and whipped cream onto two slices of pound cake when he called. It was early spring, a Sunday afternoon – slow and contemplative. Squash had dropped off a basket of early berries: small, yet bursting sweetness. Maddie prepared the crock pot with a roast, potatoes, carrots, and seasonings earlier that morning and let it simmer to perfection while she attended church with Stu. She invited him over for a meal on the rare occasions that neither was on call at the hospital. Maddie was not a "cook," did not have an ardent love for culinary arts, but she knew how to prepare simple dishes. Squash saw to that. Maddie remembered teenage days detained in the kitchen while Squash imparted wisdom.

She picked up a pound cake from Lollie's the day before. Everyone knew Lollie made the best pound cake – firm, but moist with a hint of lemon. Charlene had not even attempted to compete. That was an off-limits item, never to grace her catering list, or anyone else's in a 20-mile radius of Wynee, for that matter.

Maddie licked the cream off her fingers and picked up the phone.

"Maddie?"

"Guy?"

"How are you?"

Air exited her lungs. Undigested pot roast stirred.

Guy? It had been months. She had not seen him or heard his voice. From snippets of Wyneean conversation, she learned he left (no one knew exactly to where, but they speculated vastly just the same) and then he was back, and then he was gone again. The media had long nailed Guy's career as just another Hollywood tragedy. A shooting star that left no remnant. Another Montgomery Cliff. People needed something to talk about in Wynee, and they deliberated over the whereabouts of their once-celebrated resident. Maddie paid no attention. She prayed for his safety, deliverance out of self-loathing. She anticipated a "For Sale" sign in the wilderness that had once been the Butts's quirky, but resplendent yard.

As she closed the door on that last encounter with Guy, she resolved to be there for him if he called to her. Reaching out was done. Fretting finished. There was no debt owed him – no obligation to her childhood friend. If Lawrence's letter failed to rouse, nothing she did would. She expected his eventual and permanent departure from Wynee. She would never encounter him again, and a shadowy poignancy would linger into her aging years.

"I'm ... uh ... fine, Guy. How are you? Are you here ... in Wynee?"

"Yes. And I need to ask you something."

"Okay."

"Will you ride with me somewh ... well, I'd, uh, really like to show you something. Will you drive me somewhere? I ...

still can't drive. Mater … Matt's been driving me to the airport and some other places when I need him to. I just want to show you something, Maddie."

"I don't know, Guy." Neck muscles constricted.

"Maddie … please. I know I'm asking a lot after all this time and after the way I've treated you. Please. It's important. I'm at my parent's house."

"I'm finishing a meal with a friend right now, Guy, but maybe we can go in an hour or so. I'll ask him."

Maddie lay the phone on the kitchen counter and walked into the dining room. "It's Guy on the phone."

"Really?" said Stu.

"He wants me to drive him somewhere later. Wants to show me something. Are you okay with that?"

Stu's smile warmed her instantly, easing some of the jitters caused by the unexpected call. "Of course. There isn't any reason why it shouldn't be, right?" He winked at her. "This is the first time he's contacting you. He probably just wants to make amends. Does he sound okay?"

She nodded her head. "Just unsure of himself. It probably took a lot for him to call. I'll be right back."

She returned to the phone and told Guy she would pick him up in an hour and a half. That would give them a few more hours of daylight, in case he wanted to show her something outdoors.

"Okay. Good," was all he said before hanging up.

Disconcerted, Maddie carried the desserts into the dining room. Stu smiled and dove in, finishing cake and berries in a succession of five bites. Maddie regarded the enticing treat, but felt as if something were wedged in her throat, preventing her from even managing a taste. She stared at the plate – fork in hand.

"Lost your appetite?"

"Sort of. I'm just perplexed. I ran into Matt the other day, and he told me he's been driving Guy back and forth to the airport in Myrtle Beach. I didn't ask him why. I just figured he was making arrangements to move away somewhere. The end."

"What you're really telling me is that you were hoping that he was making arrangements to move somewhere so that you wouldn't have to think about him sad and alone holed up in that big house," he gloated.

She punched at his arm playfully. "How do you do that? I can't figure out for a second what's going on in that mind of yours!"

"Talent! Pure talent."

She shook her head and looked down at her dessert, poking it with her fork.

"Now, if you're not going to partake in that, I'd like to do the honorable thing and take it off your hands," said Stu.

She slid the dessert in front of him, which he devoured in seconds.

"I saw Matt for only a minute the other day, but he said something to me as he was walking away that made me wonder. He said, 'He's comin' back to life again.' I tried to get him to tell me what he meant by that, but he just waved me off and said he'd have to talk to me some other time."

"Well, that sounds encouraging, at least," said Stu, wiping a bit of whipped cream from the corner of his mouth. "And with him contacting you after all this time …" Stu considered Maddie for a moment as she gazed at nothing. He continued: "He's endured some major storms. Now maybe he's beginning to see the clouds departing."

"Okay. Enough of that!" said Maddie, playfully punching him again in the arm as she stood to take his plate.

"What? What did I say?" he smiled up at her.

"Enough with the weather metaphors. It's unnerving when you suddenly wax poetic. Stick to being practical, doc, or you're going to muddle me," she said, lightly.

After the dishes were in the dishwasher and Stu kissed and hugged her goodbye, Maddie got into her car and drove the short distance to Guy's house. In those sparse minutes, she measured Stu's reaction to Guy's call. *Indifference or confidence?* She was not clear where she stood with him – where she wanted to stand. There was a comfort level. They were certainly more than friends. Was their stationary relationship her fault? Were her feelings interned by memories?

Squash and her team of local boys had taken over the task of yard maintenance at the Butts's the previous summer and returned dense landscaping to its former glory. But with the return of fall's busyness – school for the boys and another family with two young children for Squash to fret over – tulips and daffodils still bloomed in abundance in beds lining the driveway, but they competed with invasive weeds. Masses of azaleas revealed color among misshapen hedges and uncontainable English ivy.

Guy sat at the oak kitchen table as Maddie hesitantly approached the back screened door. He motioned her inside. The newspaper spread before him and a glass half full of iced tea beaded with condensation in his hand. Always the physician, she absorbed his condition: his beard, which helped hide some scarring, was trimmed neatly, as was his hair; although still thinner than he should be, some weight gain was evident.

He stood gingerly, grabbed an expandable black hiking stick and a white tube lying in one of the chairs at the table, and said simply: "Thank you for coming, Maddie." She watched him limp toward the door and down the back steps to her car. He eased into the passenger seat with some effort and said nothing to her until she backed out of the driveway.

"Remember Tara?"

"What?" she asked, pulling the car to the side of the road to await instructions.

"Tara … pharaoh's palace … whatever we decided to pretend it was. Remember that old plantation we found and played at when we were kids?"

"Yes."

"Do you remember where it is?"

"Yes."

"Please driver there."

"We can't drive there. There is no exposed road, remember?" Skeptical, she added: "What's this about, Guy?"

He answered pleadingly, "Maddie, please just drive in that direction. I don't want to get into anything right now. I promise I'll tell you when we get there."

She drove to where the town of Wynee ended and the marsh began. She breathed through the queasy irritant in her stomach and squelched the fused ire/woe rising in her.

"Drive up this little road," Guy directed. "Now, turn here. Good. Just pull over in that grassy area there, and we'll walk the rest of the way."

Maddie looked at Guy, bewildered. He opened the door and lifted himself out of the car, grasping the door's frame. He expanded the metal hiking stick and steadied himself. He grabbed the white tube and shut the car door.

"You're going to *walk* the rest of the way? It's a little bit of a path to those old ruins. Is that where we're going?

"I can make it," he said. "Been doing it."

"What's this about, Guy?"

Question unheeded, Maddie stared at the woods he hobbled toward. The image of him standing on the steps of the crumbling mansion shouting, "I am Moses! I come to free my people!" vividly sprung to mind. The scene quieted vexation within.

He limped along. The trail seemed narrower, shorter – the length of half a football field and they were there. What seemed miles when they were children, was a short stroll as an adult. Surveyor flags marked an area surrounding the mansion's footprint – encroaching wilderness newly maintained.

"Come on, Maddie. He brightened, and his distorted pace quickened to an off-kilter jaunt. He made his way toward the entrance of the forgotten home.

Though marred by time and invaded by nature, the antebellum mansion – what was left of it – invoked reverence. Maddie absorbed the scene: remnants of massive columns, a portion of a stone archway, granite steps. Great oaks at each corner towered soldier-like, guarding the property with ghostly appendages of death-gray moss.

Guy lay the white tube on what remained of the front porch's landing, a thick marble slab – defiled by age – yet still distinguishable as a captivating piece of stone. Spent from the short walk, Guy lowered himself onto a massive granite step. He turned toward Maddie and watched her surveying the setting, knowing her mind reached for the same shared memories that mesmerized him when he revisited the site months earlier. The place fashioned fragments of their childhood; now it would define his future.

She realized his observation and met it with her own. He looked at home on that step – content, absolved. Her brow relaxed; the noon meal settled.

He extended a hand, an invitation. She moved thoughtfully toward him and sat next to him on the step. He looked at her for a moment and then at what had been the front yard of the property. Without glancing back at Maddie, he found her hand and held it. Silence for a moment; he kept his eyes fixed ahead.

Then he inhaled and began: "First of all … I want to tell you that I'm sorry, Maddie. From the depths of me … I'm sorry. And before you become doubtful, there is not a shred of acting in me right now. I am seriously and profoundly sorry. *For everything*. From ditching our friendship when I left here to polluting it again after the accident. I am sorry for the way I've acted, for the things I've said, and mostly … for what I've done."

Guy turned to her. Maddie studied the face forever changed by recklessness, but still her friend's face. It seemed a sincere face. Warmth permeating from his hand expressed his solemnity.

"Everything you've ever said to me … everything you've ever done for me has been right, Maddie. I'm the one who has been wrong … so wrong. I'm so sorry for the way I must have hurt you. I've thought a lot about what you told me, Maddie. I've read Daddy's letter over and over again. I've even been reading out of his old Bible. I've been able to *see* it all … see what it all means."

He paused, rubbing gently her hand reposed in his. "Is it possible for you to forgive me, Maddie? I would like … more than anything … to *know* your friendship again … to know that I have your friendship, again. I'm not certain of anything, Maddie, but I've become certain of one thing. We were supposed to be friends and we *are* supposed to be friends. Things just aren't right without it."

These were wrought words, crafted from anguish and repentance. In a gesture that needed no more thought, Maddie wiped an escaping tear, lifted her hand from his, and placed it on his scarred cheek. She smiled and gasped a sob before wrapping her arms around his neck. He yielded to her embrace. In an instant, they were pirates trespassing on a shrimp boat, rubber boot-clad crab collectors, walkers across Egypt. Ages of distress dissipated.

Gradually, the hold released and Maddie smiled through moisture. She wiped her face with the sleeve of her shirt.

"Enough of the dramatics," he said, shaking off sentiment. Maddie noticed a glint of his former self revealed in his eyes.

"Do you think I brought you out here just for melodrama? I have something to show you, as I explained on the phone."

He stood, walked to the marble step, pulled a roll of papers from the white tube, and spread them out, using a few broken pieces of marble to hold down the corners. The plans were titled, in blue ink, Exodus Productions. Expertly drawn was an architect's rendition of a stately structure flanked by oaks, interior rooms marked "editing," "office," "meetings," and massive warehouse-like buildings with antebellum facades.

"I bought it," said Guy, animated. "I've been out to California a few times lately to tie up some loose ends with my agent and to do some research about the business aspects of movie production. I've bought all this land, the house, everything around here. Took some doing – tracking down owners, skirting around historians and environmentalists, but I did it. I'm starting a production company and this is going to be a studio. I'm going to promote this area to Hollywood for Southern-themed movies."

He paused; he was 10 again, eager for Maddie to be impressed. But she was contemplative, studying the plans.

"What do you think?" he asked anxiously, impatient for approval. "I'm not going back to Hollywood – unless I need to be there for meetings. I'm staying here and making movies instead of starring in them." He rattled on, filling her silence:

"It's less expensive to make movies here. This site's perfect. It all just started taking shape one day when I was thinking about us as kids. And I ran into Squash, and you know how she can just say the oddest, but most profound things. She told me to cast my net … *cast my net*. Didn't wrap my head around that one for days. But then … Come on, Maddie, say *something*."

She lifted her gaze from the meticulous plans and acknowledged him. No pretending; no play acting. Guy Olivier Rhett Butts was before her, rehabilitated – *running the race with endurance*. Vibrant green duck weed blankets muddied waters.

Maddie smiled at her friend's anticipation. "I think you're well on your way, Moses."

T H E   E N D

Deena Bouknight lived in the Western North Carolina mountains for 10 years and now resides in South Carolina with her husband and two children. She is a freelance writer, contributing to regional, national, and international publications for more than 30 years. This is her second novel. Her first: *Broken Shells*. She has written a children's book, *A Wintry Day Walk*, and contributed to three books: *Portraits of Grace*, *Humor for a Sister's Heart*, and *Big Book of Christmas Joy*. She is also a teacher of literature and writing.

Deena was inspired to write *Playing Guy* because of a "sense of place," described by Henry David Thoreau, gleaned from the ruins of Sheldon Church near Beaufort, S.C., and by this passage from <u>The Narrative of the Captivity and Restoration of Mary Rowlandson:</u> *"The portion of some is to have their afflictions by drops, now one drop and then another; but the dregs of the cup, the wine of astonishment, like a sweeping rain that leaveth no food, did the Lord prepare to be my portion. Affliction I wanted, and affliction I had, full measure (I thought) and pressed down and running over. Yet I see, when God calls a person to anything, and through never so many difficulties, yet He is fully able to carry them through and make them see, and say they have been gainers thereby."*

Made in the USA
Columbia, SC
28 July 2019